WESTMINSTER PUBLIC LIBRARY

3 3020 01099 3532

Lyz Kelley CH

ATONEMENT

A Lonely Ridge Collection Novel

D1031451

DISCARD

Westminster Public Library
3705 W 112th Ave
Westminster, CO 80031
www.westminsterlibrary.org

BELVITRI SERVICES, LLC
Littleton, Colorado
ISBN: 978-0-9972582-9-5

Atonement
Copyright © 2018 Lyz Kelley

All rights reserved.
Copyright invigorates creativity, encourages diversity, promotes
and supports free speech.
Thank you for buying an authorized edition of this book and for
complying with the copyright laws by not printing, scanning, uploading,
or sharing any part of this book without permission of the publisher. If
you would like to use material from this book (other than for review
purposes), prior written permission must be obtained by contacting the
publisher Belvitri Services, LLC at or by writing to Belvitri.com or the
following address:
8357 N. Rampart Range Rd. Unit 106-114
Littleton, CO 80125
This is a work of fiction. Names, characters, places or incidents are
either the product of the author's imagination or are used fictitiously,
and any resemblance to the actual persons, living or dead, business
establishments, events or locales is entirely coincidental.

For questions and comments about the quality of this book please
contact us at LyzKelley.com

From award-winning author, Lyz Kelley...

Riches to rags. Does the murderer's daughter deserve a second chance?

The FBI has convicted Rachelle's father, and her hometown is reeling from the corruption. She's hoping to rebuild her life, and the last thing she expects to find is help from a super-sexy video gamer geek.

Entrepreneur Jacob has escaped to Colorado for a much-needed rest before developing his next game world. He's looking for inspiration in the mountain valley, not expecting an interior designer to get his creative juices flowing.

When Jacob asks Rachelle to redesign his vacation home, she has no idea she's headed deeper into a world of jealousy and manipulation. But she's a survivor, and swears she will never trust anyone again. Can Jacob provide her a soft place to land until she discovers there's no better place to call home than the small-town of Elkridge?

The ELKRIDGE SERIES debuts a quirky cast of beloved characters. If you like a sensual romance, deep emotional topics, and a cozy happy ending then ATONEMENT is for you.

Get your copy today and immerse yourself in the Colorado small town.

More Books By
Lyz Kelley

BLINDED
SPURNED
ABANDONED
ORPHANED
EXPOSED
RESCUED

UNMISTAKEN
ATONEMENT

Coming Soon...
BITTERSWEET

The Molly Award for Excellence

"A writer who will go the distance."

"Masterful dialog."

"I look forward to seeing this book on the bookshelves."

The Sheila Finalist

"The story has great bones! The plot is interesting, the characters are unique...there are so many things to love about this story."

"H & H are both very appealing and certainly not cookie cutter characters."

"Your opening is a grabber."

"This is one of the best books I've read in a good long while. CONGRATULATIONS."

"Prose is sleek, polished and smooth, a near frictionless read."

The Marlene Finalist

"You have a lovely writing style with dialogue and scene setting."

"The sensory details are rich, and I was able to visualize the scenes. I chuckled several times at your turn of phrase and thought they were very sassy and smart."

"The plot seems to have it all: conflict, a mystery and a romance. So kudos for creating an interesting story."

Dear Reader,

Thank you for picking up Atonement.

I wrote this book for those in the world who are survivors. Those who have lost and had to start over, or those who must keep on living after a loss.

Life is hard. It's unfair. And there often are no answers to the question why.

When I was a kid, I was angry about bad stuff going on in my life. For years, I remained closed off, pushed people away, and let the negative fester.

Later I discovered I didn't even like who I was, and have worked hard to change. Today I try my best to look beyond the negativity of the moment, toward the light of the future. And if I encounter anger or meanness, I have more tolerance, and I try my best not to judge.

I have failed, many times, and that's okay. I'm human. I believe we all, every single one of us, have what it takes to be hero—a survivor. It's a state of mind, and one I take to heart.

So, thank you for reading this book and taking the journey towards that light with me.

I wish you all the best this day has to offer.

~ Lyz

ACKNOWLEDGEMENTS

There is a tribe of people I need to thank for helping me with the technical aspects of this book.

First Tina Marie Bisiaux, MS, MAC, LADC-S and Derek Shihan for helping with the co-dependent and substance abuse emotional arcs for the user and those who love them. Very powerful stuff.

Second, to Sean for your help with the gaming and LGBTQ aspects of my story. Julia Freewoman, aka the Resident Geek for pushing me to stretch my gaming imagination.

Aidy Award for allowing me to bounce plot ideas around, and to Faith Freewoman, my fantastic editor, who worked tirelessly to make the best book possible. For Carol Agnew, who crossed every T and dotted every I.

Melody Simmons who created an excellent cover for my story.

The Kelley's Heroes for spotting last minute typos and inconsistencies. You have my sincere gratitude.

~Lyz

Chapter One

"What idiot put these instructions together?" Rachelle slid the sheet of nonsense closer, then looked at the set of electrical cords.

Of course the black wires weren't marked. And the labeled pictures didn't help either. Rachelle rubbed her temples, trying to hold off the thumping ache.

"Why does everything have to be so hard?"

She rocked back on her heels and looked around the twelve-hundred-square-foot space. Gone was the original oil painting of an Indian chief. Gone were the handcrafted pool table and bar. Gone were all the artistic pieces the creative side of her loved. The furnishings she spent years collecting to design the perfect home for her father, all gone—seized by the government as punishment for her father's sins.

Her father's arrest for drug trafficking, tax evasion, and a couple dozen more offenses, forced her out of the only home she'd ever known and into the position of having to take the first job available. She hated turning her beloved entertainment room into a sterile video gaming theatre, but she couldn't pretend she was fasting anymore.

She might have been proud of the six-figure makeover if the new job hadn't forced her to work in the one place she never wanted to see again. The place she'd worked hard to make perfect, both to avoid her father's anger, all while providing a safe home for her and her brother.

The modern chrome and leather chairs and floor-to-ceiling screen created a theatre of imagination, and ensured the new owner had no distractions—that was the idea, anyway. Jacob Reye's assistant, Ben, said the owner wanted a place where he could relax, rejuvenate, and create.

Unfortunately, life wasn't a day at the spa.

The sparse furnishing reminded her just how empty her life had become. Life had given her such a hard shake, her world ended up broken into tiny, unrecognizable pieces. Add in a couple of weeks to move, plus a couple of months to realize her old life had evaporated before her eyes, and what she ended up with *was* a bunch of nothing.

She pressed her elbows into the steel grey wool carpet to study the ultra-modern game chairs the shipping company delivered that morning.

"Whoever invented these things should be shot."

The ergonomics of the design were off, as well as the functionality. But she wouldn't complain—to the owner anyway. She was just happy to have the work.

"Do you need help?" A voice as deep and smooth as her dark roast coffee ambled its way into the room.

Her heart gave a little leap of surprise. On all fours, she rotated to look at the intruder. "Who are you? The construction work is done. Nobody should be in here."

When he didn't answer, she repositioned to see him more clearly.

He didn't appear threatening, but held her gaze for several heartbeats, a frown pulling at the edge of his mouth. He studied her some more, then shifted sideways to see what she'd been working on. "I see my chairs have arrived."

Your chairs? Ooops. She hadn't recognized Jacob Reyes, CEO and founder of Exlander Force, from photographs she found with a Google search. Right now his hair was mussed, and he hadn't shaved. The stubble set the tone for his sexy, bad-boy style, but then the loose-fitting jeans and flip-flops left the geeky in place.

However, the video game guru and multimillionaire standing in the doorway was much more than his digital images.

His attention flicked from the chairs back to her face.

When the scrutiny became too uncomfortable, she got to her feet as gracefully as she could manage. "You must be the new owner." She straightened her blouse and smoothed back her hair—which, like everything else in her life, had spun out of control.

"Oh, yeah, sorry. I'm Jacob. I take it you're the interior designer Ben's been raving about."

She'd take the compliment, if for no other reason than she'd need references later. Right now all she wanted to do was finish this job and finally, completely write "the end" to this chapter of her life. Every day she remained in the place added to the continuously looped heartache.

"That's nice of Ben to say." She considered the grey walls and the brushed stainless-steel bar. The design had come together better than expected, but the entertainment room missed the feminine touches she liked to add. The décor exuded masculinity, just like the owner. "I'm glad you like it."

"Like it?" His eyes darkened. "It's like you read my mind. It's perfect. Better than I imagined."

Relief eased the knot in her stomach. At least Jacob wasn't as hard to please as her father.

She slammed the door on the memory, refusing to think about the psychopath who'd turned her world inside out. "I'm sure you'll want to look around, so I'll get out of your way. Just let me know when I should come back."

"Wait." He reached out a hand as she walked by, then caught himself. "It looks like you're almost finished." He pointed toward the chairs. "I have another set of these chairs in San Diego, and I learned the hard way that they can be a little tricky to put together since the instructions are missing a few steps."

Tell me about it.

He leaned in a little closer. "We can knock out the setup before Ben gets back with lunch. How about it?"

"I spoke to your assistant this morning. I thought he was in California."

"He was. We just landed an hour ago. I came along to see how the new design is coming and sneak in a mini vacation."

"Do you always fly with your assistants?"

She cringed, knowing the answer was none of her business. But she was curious.

Based on the video calls, Ben was in his mid to late twenties and had a body made for magazine covers. His rapid-fire approach to things gave the impression he was always in a hurry to be somewhere else, and could be a bit overwhelming. He switched topics probably as often as he changed wardrobes. However, she admired his bold charm. He lived out loud and real. He didn't hide his personality and was the type of real she'd never been allowed to be.

Jacob chuckled. "No. I don't travel with my assistants. Ben's my half-brother."

Brother? Wow, she didn't pick up on the family relationship, and his openness startled her, although both were refreshing. She hesitated a second, letting the information settle.

A hint of a smile tugged at the corners of Jacob's mouth, like he wasn't surprised by her assumptions. His eyes flickered with a hint of humor.

"It's not always easy working with family," she offered, to explain her weird reaction.

"No." He leaned a little closer, like he wanted to tell her a secret. "It's not."

She didn't move back. She just let her senses take in his masculine scent, which reminded her of a coastal breeze. An image of him standing on a sailboat, the wind in his hair and his tanned face tilted toward the sun, stole into her mind along with his scent, an image that matched the smooth timbre of his voice.

She let his masculinity wash over her until her apprehension receded, but not the magnetic pull. She'd been around his type most of her life and should be wary, but for some reason, he'd sneaked in under her radar.

"Maybe I should just let you get on with your day." She gripped the stair railing tighter. "I'm assuming putting the chairs together can wait." With a handful of misgivings, she climbed out of the self-imposed trap. Slowly ascending the staircase, she peeked over her shoulder at the sailor man.

Sure enough, he was staring with such focus, her breath hitched in her throat. He wasn't dangerous...at least she didn't think so...but he had an intensity about him.

"Is there something else you need, Mr. Reyes?"

"Jacob," he reminded gently. He stood at the bottom of the stairs with one foot on the bottom step. "I have a proposition for you."

She clutched the stairwell to stop her feet from skedaddling in the opposite direction.

Hosting parties for her father had normally resulted in a variety of indecent propositions. She'd been on display, like a cow in an auction ring waiting for the highest bidder.

Jacob Reyes needed to make the next move.

She waited to see where he headed with his proposal, and slipped seamlessly into her disinterested pose—a mental state to establish distance and guard against evoking a reaction. Powerful men liked to dominate and chase, like a wolf tracking a rabbit. She'd do nothing to stimulate his carnal instincts. To outsmart his offers of diamonds, trips, cars, and whatnot, she needed to analyze his approach, and counter it.

Then again, his offer might be decent.

But she couldn't take the chance. She'd survived this long by being careful.

She'd never again be for sale to the highest bidder.

"And what are you offering?" She lifted her chin a bit higher and squeezed her shoulder blades together.

"Since you nailed what I was looking for in this room, I was wondering if you'd be willing to redesign the rest of the house."

Oh, God no. Her next breath got stuck halfway to her throat. He had no idea he was crushing her heart, but he was doing an excellent job.

Her mind whirled with dozens of reasons why she shouldn't touch a project like this, and there was only one reason to do it, and it trumped all others.

Money.

The government had frozen her family's assets. She'd never quite understood the value of a robust bank account until she had nothing.

She let out a self-conscious chuckle, hoping to cover her trepidation. "That is a nice offer, Jacob."

"But?"

She clung to the railing to keep her hands from shaking. "But it would take months to redesign the whole house, and I can't commit to such a large project."

He proceeded up the stairs, his head down, his frown hardening. As she suspected, he wasn't the type to take no for an answer. She braced to hold her ground, refusing to be the compliant daughter anymore. She was free. Free to choose the next step. At least that's what she kept telling herself.

"I'll pay you well."

I'm not for sale. "I'll pass," she responded without taking a breath.

He stopped a step below where she stood. "There are very few designers who can transform a room the way you did, Ms. Clairemont. You have a unique talent. One which needs to be showcased, and I intend for this home to be a designer's dream—magazine coverage and all. If it's not about the money, maybe it's about the challenge. So, what do you say?"

Trust me, it's not me you want.

She locked her knees to keep herself from jumping at the chance to create with abandon. To mix textures and colors and styles. To live out loud. To have her designs published in a magazine. Oh, so tempting. "Mr. Reyes, your offer is intriguing, but I have another job starting tomorrow." *At least I hope I can find something.*

The fear of the unknown again pressed in.

His face wilted before blooming into the most glorious smile. "How does three million dollars and six months sound? And for you, a hundred grand for your time."

A hundred grand, as in a hundred thousand?

She choked. How could she turn down a job doing what she loved?

She could tell he sensed her hesitation, because his glowing enthusiasm continued to spread across his entire face.

Caution rolled over her as easily as scented body lotion. She could smell and feel it sinking into her skin.

She needed the money, but was working for a stranger...a guy who was clearly loaded with cash...just another tempting trap? Plus, she didn't want to redesign her childhood home. The eight-thousand-square-foot, six-bedroom mansion had been stylishly decorated until her father destroyed everything with his greed.

She needed to avoid getting caught in another gilded cage. The same cage her father snared her in using family obligations and money and social standing. She wouldn't be ambushed by a man—never, ever, ever again.

"Your offer is very generous, but—"

"Don't turn me down just yet. Think about it for a few days."

With a whoosh, her tension drained away, leaving her mollified. She could call in a few days and tell him she'd secured another job—any job.

The angles of his face softened, except for the dimple in his whiskered cheeks. "Can I tempt you to stay for lunch?"

He moved closer. Way too close.

She should leave, but he smelled delicious, like a day on the beach, the wind in her hair, and sand beneath her toes. She understood the risk of being too close to a man, but she couldn't move.

"What do you say?"

A nervous chuckle slipped out, and her cheeks heated. "I'm sure you want to get settled in your new home."

The quick tapping of footsteps on the upper floor announced the arrival of Ben. "Hi, Rachelle. Are you staying for lunch?"

"Well, I..." Why was she hesitating? She shouldn't be hesitating. She gestured toward the top of the stairs. "I need to get going."

Jacob gave her a slow, confident smile, the kind that took just long enough for her to wonder whether she should even consider helping him redesign her home— well, his home, now.

He was gorgeous in a messy, bad-boy geek kind of way, and she wished her heart hadn't decided to do a workout at that very moment.

Ben disappeared to answer a ringing phone.

"I'll be here for a week before I need to head back to California, in case you change your mind."

"Thank you for your offer, but I won't change my mind."

She couldn't deal with him—the guy who knew how to make a pair of worn-out jeans and a formfitting T-shirt skimming over a toned torso look sexy. Weren't gamers supposed to be reclusive and on the pale, skinny, glasses-wearing side, never having seen the light of day? Not tanned and built like a Grecian god.

She picked up her purse, and he followed. "If you're

not interested in lunch, how about we get together for dinner tomorrow?"

Dinner? He wasn't asking her out on a date...was he? "I don't think it's a good idea. I don't like to mix business with—"

"Pleasure?" His attention dropped to her mouth and lingered way too long. "I don't know anyone in town, and I was hoping for some company. You know, pizza, beer, something casual. Besides, we can finish putting those chairs together."

Oh, yeah, those stupid chairs.

His pizza offer seemed legit. Dinner only. No bed sports. If it wasn't legit, he hid his intentions well.

If he'd offered her French cuisine or the best cut of Kobe beef, she'd have turned him down flat. But pizza...thick, warm dough, covered by melted cheese...what wasn't to like? She couldn't remember the last time she had a slice of pizza. Phillip, the gourmet chef her father hired, would have been horrified. Even if she had asked for pizza, it was considered junk food, and would have never been permitted. Everything in her life had been measured, weighed, and organized—down to her daily calorie count.

"Sounds nice." The words slipped out before her brain engaged.

"Jacob?" Ben interrupted.

She swallowed to moisten her dry mouth. She'd lost her chance to retract the acceptance.

Ben appeared again at the top of the stairs, waving a phone at Jacob. "It's Larson. He's got a problem."

"Of course he has a problem." Jacob's facial features hardened, and became unreadable. "I'll be there in a minute." He attempted to recover his smile. "I need to take this. How about tomorrow around six?"

"I...ah...sure." She glanced over her shoulder. "You'd better take your call."

He nodded with a puff of frustration. "Right," he said,

although he seemed somewhat reluctant to move. "Thank you for your hard work. It's perfect," he left her with a hearty serving of praise, something she'd rarely experienced in her life.

However, she wasn't sure she agreed with his appraisal.

The masculine, metal-grey design was nothing she'd ever tried before, and now that she'd met Jacob, the cold tones of the room didn't seem to match the playful undertones of his personality. Odd how her father wanted to be surrounded by wood and fresh flowers and beautiful pieces of art when he'd destroyed so many things—like her.

He'd crushed her true nature, bullied and punished her until she was little more than a windup doll, and she obeyed because it was the only way to endure in a world that wasn't of her making.

But now she had a plan.

She was determined to become a person even she liked being around.

Chapter Two

Jacob accepted the phone from Ben and walked out the double sliding glass doors to look at the mountain range spanning the horizon. He closed his eyes against the bright sun.

"Larson, what's up?"

"Hey, buddy." The slurred words meant only one thing. Larson was high.

The time Jacob locked Larson in their dorm room and stayed with him for a week to get his strung-out buddy sober hit him in the chest like a sledgehammer.

"Where are you?" Jacob bent his head and lowered his voice, his protectiveness kicking in.

"Dude, I'm at the beach. The waves are so cool. They go in and out and in and out. You should come see."

A rush of relief almost made him dizzy. At least Larson hadn't gotten on a plane. The last time, his buddy couldn't remember where he'd landed. Finding him had taken eighteen excruciating hours and dealing with authorities in multiple countries.

"What's with you? Why are you getting stoned? You promised never again."

"Take it easy. I'm just having a little fun."

"Is anyone with you?" Jacob turned to see Ben hovering in the doorway.

A woman giggled in the background. Jacob closed his eyes to gather patience. "Larson? Are you there?"

"Yeah, man. I'm here."

"Okay. Stay put." Jacob lowered the phone and

switched to his friend finder to locate his business partner.

Coronado Beach.

He texted Courtney, Larson's substance abuse counselor, a quick SOS text.

"I'm sending help."

"No need. I'm good—oh, shit."

"Larson? Larson are you there?" Jacob shoved his fingers into his hair and gripped the strands, tugging hard, while he listened to rustling and muttering in the background.

Then he straightened, dropped a hand, and let his thumbs dance across the keys. He re-read the text and pressed send. A couple of seconds later the texted response, "I'm on my way," appeared.

The pressure pinching the base of his skull released.

"Larson, Courtney's on her way. Do me a favor and don't give her a hard time, okay?"

"Love you, man."

Part of him wanted to return the sentiment, but the empathetic, emotional bridge between them burned down when Larson showed up to a staff meeting totally bombed. "Okay, buddy. Just let Courtney drive you home, okay?"

The call ended with no warning.

"Shit." Jacob held the phone to his head, feeling the cool glass against his skin.

"You know he'll continue to get worse," Ben said. "He's got money now, and too much time on his hands."

"He shouldn't have any extra time. He promised to send me a new world design last week. The capital investors want a meeting."

"But he didn't send the designs, did he?"

Jacob studied his brother, who was leaning casually against the sliding glass doorframe. "This is just a slipup. He went to see Courtney a couple of days ago. She'll straighten him out. She did the last time."

Courtney, a psych major, used to live across the hall in their coed dorm. She figured out pretty quickly why Jacob had handcuffed Larson to the bed in their room, and offered to help Jacob take shifts...and was still, years later, taking shifts, trying to help Larson learn to take responsibility and stay clean.

Ben crossed his arms, his face posting an "are you kidding me?" sign. "When will you stop covering and taking responsibility for everyone else?"

Jacob, intent on ignoring his brother, slashed a finger across the phone's screen to watch Courtney's little blue dot drift toward the beach. Larson's drug counselor, who should be described as a friend after all the therapy work she'd been doing with him over the years, would make sure he didn't get into trouble. Larson was safe. At least for now.

He looked at Ben and shrugged. "It's just what I do. Besides, this is partially my fault. I should have talked Larson into setting up a trust. Then he wouldn't have cash readily available. A large wad of money in the hands of a recovering addict is too tempting."

His brother produced the combo eye-roll-brow-raise, and added a phhffft, but chose not to add to the heaping pile of guilt. "Yeah, like it's your fault he checked into the San Diego Fairmont and trashed the place."

"At least he picked somewhere exclusive. The manager agreed to keep the mess out of the papers as long as I paid for all the damages."

"He's lucky he wasn't arrested."

Ben had a point. Considering the number of drugs and prostitutes he had with him, Larson would have been facing some serious jail time. Jacob passed Ben and entered the open kitchen, stopping to study the vaulted ceilings. The large room had more cabinets than a locker room. "Did you find something for us to eat?"

"This town is smaller than a closet. There isn't much, but I think I can manage." Ben zipped across the room to open the refrigerator. "How about I make your favorite? Mac and cheese."

Thank God for comfort food. The growing tension at the base of his neck eased. "By the way, I asked Rachelle to dinner tomorrow night. I promised her pizza."

Ben paused while pulling a pan from one of the cupboards. "Good thing I like you, 'cause there isn't a pizza joint in this town." Ben moved to the sink to fill the pan with water. "Meat lovers?"

"And maybe a margarita. I'm not sure what she likes to eat." Jacob leaned his hip against the counter. "I asked if she would design the rest of the house. She turned me down."

"Really? That's odd."

"That's what I thought." Her rejection plus Larson's escalating drug problem added daunting complexities to his already bulging bag of responsibilities.

"That woman has talent." Ben found a bag of pasta shells in one of the myriad cabinets. "What did you offer her?"

"I offered her a hundred grand, plus a magazine spread giving her the credit."

"That's more than fair."

Jacob stared at his brother. "Yet she still turned me down. Maybe I should have offered her more."

"No, you shouldn't offer her more. You'd give the shirt off your back if you thought it would help someone." Ben waved him off. "Try being selfish for once, and stop thinking about everyone else."

"She's really good. You were right. She understands what I want, and delivers. That's gotta be worth something."

Ben opened one of the two refrigerators, taking out package after package of cheese from the inner drawer. "Of course she did. You went over the specs a hundred times."

"But only after she came up with the initial design. Did

you see her sketches?"

Ben's forehead crinkled. "They didn't look different from any one of the thousands of storyboards you get from the game designers every day."

He rejected his brother's confusion. There was a difference...subtle, yes, but it was there. Something made the room come into 3D focus. "Still. I like what she put together."

"I don't know why you bought this place. It's so"—Ben flipped his hand back and forth like he was waving away a heavy dose of cologne—"out of the way."

"You do know why I bought it. The tax accountant said I should invest in real estate. Calgary is too far away, and Colorado reminds me of home. The government was selling this place for a steal, and I couldn't resist. Besides, I want a place to think."

"Pfft." Ben blew out some more attitude. "If you wanted quiet, you got your wish. If you listen closely, you can hear the earth rotating."

"Good thing you're not staying the whole week." Jacob returned the attitude. "Ross will be happy to have you home. He's only texted you a hundred times today."

"You're just jealous because you don't have a squeeze. I could get you one, you know. There are a dozen women who would die to be your date any night of the week."

Ben threw him a look filled with a heap of pity, but his concern was misplaced. Jacob didn't need a woman in his life. He had Ben and Larson, and dozens of programmers who depended on him for work so they could safely go home to their families every night. "Stop worrying about me."

"I do worry about you. You're not happy."

Maybe he wasn't happy, but he was trying to be content, and not fight so hard to get his father's attention.

He'd made his point.

The twelve million in his bank account should prove something, yet he wasn't quite sure what. That he was a better programmer than his father? That he had a better head for business? That he knew how to make things happen?

"I'll be a lot happier when I come up with an idea for my new game world. I keep hoping a brilliant and unusual idea will come to me, but so far everything's been kinda lame."

"That's not what I'm talking about, and you know it."

"I've got a great life. A business. Houses. Cars. An airplane I partially own. I'm good with what I have—why wouldn't I be happy?"

Yet Ben was right.

Sure, he could drop a couple of grand at dinner, sit in box seats in any sports stadium, even pick up some woman and have a mindless romp with no regrets come morning, but the part he missed was someone in his life who understood his drive, his need to create. He thought Larson got it, but his buddy only cared about two things— money and drugs.

Jacob wanted more. He wanted to build something unusual, mind-blowing. Something to entertain gamers all over the world and take their minds off whatever was troubling them, at least for a little while.

The sound a kid makes when chasing a newly acquired puppy around the yard, caught Jacob's attention.

Ben was laughing at him. Jacob wasn't surprised. His brother had been with him enough years to know when he was blowing smoke out of his butt.

"Fine." Ben waved a spatula in his direction. "However, when you find the right one, please promise me you won't push her away. You tend to get single-minded when you work."

"I don't push people away," he reached into the beverage refrigerator for a beer, twisting the top in one practiced move.

He wouldn't push Rachelle away.

Visions of her on hands and knees, muttering about stupid wires and idiotic instructions came too easily. Jacob didn't quite know what to do about those luscious curves and soft, sad violet eyes. She was amazing—

"Yo, bro."

Jacob stared at his brother. "What?"

Ben tutted and turned back to the stove. "I said, you may not intend to push people away, but you do. You're a one-track-mind workaholic."

Jacob set his beer on the counter. "When you're responsible for forty-seven people, let's see if you don't work lots of hours."

"Then it's a good thing you bought this house." Ben waved the spatula like he was conducting a symphony. "You might get more than a couple of hours' sleep."

Love and concern were mapped across his sibling's face. Jacob forced a chuckle meant to ease his brother's worry lines. At the same time, he hoped his brother was right.

Sleep had eluded him for years. He was exhausted, and was looking forward to a few days to himself. Actually, that wasn't true. He wouldn't mind the company of an intriguing blonde. Rachelle was closed off, and a challenge, and he'd like to find the magical key to unlock her secrets.

Does she like living in Colorado? What's her favorite design? Does she have a boyfriend? Does she want a family?

Jacob took a long swig of beer. "We never finished our conversation from last night."

"You mean about Ross and I becoming fosters or adopting?" The spatula in Ben's hand paused, and his expression narrowed. "Why? Are you taking Dad's side?"

"Hell, no. Dad and I don't agree on anything." He picked at his beer label. "You and Ross will make great parents. I think we should start off-loading some of your responsibilities so you have more flexibility in your schedule."

"You should do something about Larson first."

The beer in his mouth launched up his nose. He coughed, and then snorted to get the liquid down. "Larson is celebrating our win. We worked hard to get the game and all the side products to market on time."

"We all worked hard. Why are you still protecting him?" The irritation in Ben's voice could have been heard in the next room.

Was he protecting Larson too much?

Maybe. Jacob shrugged. "Larson didn't have it easy growing up. His dad transferred eight times in thirteen years. Every time Larson got settled, the family would pack up again. After a while, he stopped wanting to make friends." His gut clenched.

His college roommate had disappeared again into his inner world. The abandonment hurt. Just like when his mom died. He'd lost his buddy. Now he was losing a business partner.

Drugs had turned his friend into a liability, and it was up to Jacob to fix the situation. He couldn't lose his best friend. He'd already lost his mom.

"You're not the only one he's disappointed," Ben added. "He's let his entire team down. It's better if the truth comes out."

Jacob laughed to himself, finding the statement about truth and coming out in the same conversation ironic. His brother hid his sexual identity for years, and understood better than anyone the up-and-down consequences of living the truth.

Yet Jacob heard Ben's underlying sentiment.

Jacob wasn't living his truth. He was lonely, and the beautiful designer reminded him how empty his life had become.

He shook off the look on Ben's face. "I'll be in the office if you need anything."

"I'll call when the food's ready."

Food. He was hungry, but not for dinner.

A flash of Rachelle's scrumptious hips came to mind. When she had turned around, his mind went silent. She had a face so perfect, it reminded him of polished porcelain. Her eyes were violet, like the Colorado columbine, only brighter.

Her look reminded him of Adira Cato, the warrior princess in his Exlander game. Strong. Fierce. Resourceful. But her strength wasn't what attracted him to her. It was the sadness in her eyes. The hopelessness drew him in. He understood that kind of hurt, and wondered about the cause.

He made his way out of the kitchen to let Ben weave his meal magic.

Rachelle Clairemont made his body parts take note. For the first time in months, he was hungry for a feminine touch.

The question was, what was he going to do about it?

Chapter Three

Rachelle drove her powder blue Mercedes down the narrow, curvy dirt road and stopped in front of the tiny cabin. The single-room structure barely held heat and was smaller than her bedroom at home.

Home. She had to stop calling the house on the ridge her home. It wasn't hers anymore.

She should leave Elkridge.

Find a new place and start over.

Anywhere the demons didn't creep out at night and torment her with her failings. Failings she was trying to fix.

She lifted the bag of groceries a few extra inches, retrieved her purse and the dog food, and tiptoed on her three-inch heels through the mud and weeds to the steps leading to the front door. With her hands full, she turned the knob with her fingertips and kicked the door open wide with the side of her stiletto. A flash of brindle bolted past her legs and disappeared.

"Dempsey!"

Damn dog. The next time she saw her brother she just might strangle him. The night of her father's arrest, Brad disappeared, leaving her a note to watch after Dempsey. Her brother was well aware she was scared of dogs. She'd gone to his vet clinic to give Dempsey back, but Brad had cleaned out his office and vanished.

The FBI said her younger brother hadn't been involved in the scandal, but her gut told her something quite different. She didn't want to know. Knowing only caused more trouble, and she had enough to worry about.

Rachelle dropped the bags on the counter, then turned to scan the tree line.

"Dempsey?"

Fear, anger, and frustration tangled into a monkey's fist, the kind of knot she used to make for her sailboating grandfather before he died, her mother left, her father got angry, and her life imploded.

She banged a spoon on the dog's empty bowl. "Dempsey! Dinnertime."

The deception only worked half the time. She didn't blame the brindled French bulldog for wanting his freedom.

Even after she'd been unleashed from her family, she hadn't run.

Danger was still looming.

The FBI had warned her to stick close to home in case they had more questions.

Like her sweater, she didn't dare pull at the string, otherwise her whole life would unravel. She slipped into the pair of worn clogs she scored for a dollar at a garage sale and walked down the steps. Dempsey rounded the corner with a stick in his mouth just as she touched the last stair.

"You want to play, and I never have enough energy to keep you out of trouble."

He dropped the stick by her foot.

"Okay. We'll play, but only for a few minutes. Deal?"

He tilted his head and looked at her with those big, brown eyes. He nudged the stick with his nose when she reached down, but then turned and readied himself like a racer in the starting blocks.

"Fetch." She tossed the stick, but Dempsey stopped after a few feet to stare down the road, his ears perked, his eyes focused, his nostrils pulsating in and out. He barked once in warning at the Jeep driving around the bend.

Her stomach muscles clenched. "Great." Could her day get any worse? She swallowed a giant wad of humble pie.

"Hey, Rachelle." Jenna Graden slid out of the passenger side of the blue Jeep with a sugary sweet smile. The forced expression made Rachelle's teeth ache.

Rachelle put her hand up to shade her eyes from the setting sun. "Jenna. Grant." She nodded her acknowledgement. "Are you here to gloat?"

Jenna paused. "You don't know me very well if you think I'm here to gloat."

Rachelle had met Jenna when she ordered baked goods from her bakery, but didn't know her. In fact there were very few townspeople she'd been allowed to associate with. Her father wouldn't allow her to socialize in the 'hood, as he liked to call the people living in Elkridge.

"You lived in this cabin once." She pointed at the structure only fit for overnighters. "Now you're married, and have a beautiful home and a precious little boy. I bet townspeople find me living in this place quite funny."

"I told you this was a bad idea." Jenna turned to go, but Grant caught her arm. Jenna eased back from her husband. "What? She's mad as a fly stuck in frosting. She'll never accept our help."

Grant turned to Rachelle, his eyes narrowing. "Rachelle, retract your claws. We only came to help—not judge."

Help? "Why? Neither one of you have any reason to help me. I've been nasty to you both. I don't deserve your help."

The local baker retrieved a brown cardboard box with an orange bow on top from the front seat of the Jeep. "This is for you. I boxed your favorites. There are some magic bars and brownies and a few ginger cookies."

Her favorites? Not even close, but she extended a tentative hand and accepted the gracious offering.

"Thank you," she murmured.

The familiar sting plaguing her eyes had returned. She only nodded, because anything more would cause a full-blown, bawling mess.

"I also wish to thank you, Grant, for giving me a job reference for the Reyes remodel. Without it I wouldn't have been able to pay Maggie back for allowing me to stay here."

Grant took a step closer. "If there's anyone in town who knows what you're going through, Rachelle, it's me. My mom was arrested along with your dad, but neither one of us is responsible for what happened. Both of us got caught in the rockslide of bullshit."

Jenna glared at Grant. "What my husband is trying to say is no one knew the extent of the illegal operation. It was way bigger than anyone imagined. Drugs. Trafficking in sex and babies. Who knew?"

Rachelle knew, only she had been too scared to say anything. And a lot of people got hurt. Hindsight had sliced a notch in her soul that still festered.

"I appreciate you both stopping by. I do. It's just my dad hurt a lot of people. I don't blame anyone for hating me. I don't. It will take time to make things right, and you're not doing yourselves any favors by being seen with me."

"Would you just stop feeling sorry for yourself?" Jenna marched up into her comfort zone. "Sure, you weren't always the nicest person to deal with, but today is a new day. I've seen the good side of you. It's in there, hidden by glitz and glamour, but it's still there."

Rachelle's mind clogged with denial. "How would you know?"

"You had nothing to gain by coming to my shop and telling me I should trust my husband—that he wasn't guilty of what I accused him of doing. You defended him when everyone, including me, believed him guilty. Without you, I wouldn't be married, or have a healthy, adorable son."

Grant stepped forward placing a hand on his wife's shoulder. "She's right, you know. There are other people in town willing to help, too. All you need to do is ask."

What was she supposed to say? She'd never needed to ask for help before.

The old Rachelle would have blown them off, but the new Rachelle didn't know the protocol of friendship. Before, her friends had been handpicked and were required to like her.

How did one go about making friends?

How did one make a life? Funny how only having a couple of suitcases full of clothes and a car desperately needing an oil change made you feel insecure.

"Several months ago, I was the one wanting to help this town. I was looking into purchasing that old, abandoned house by the high school."

"You mean the old Winner place?"

"That's the one. I thought it would be perfect for an after-school program. Kids get in trouble and start using drugs when they're bored." She turned to Grant. "You remember what it was like. The only place we had to hang out was the cemetery. I thought maybe if we could get everyone behind it, we could put in some computers, maybe a pool table, and I could teach some art classes."

"And maybe I could organize a baking class or two," Jenna's eyes lit up.

"How about finding someone to give skateboard lessons?" Grant added.

Jenna grabbed Grant's arm. "Karly over at Helper Shelter has been wanting to teach kids how to train dogs."

"And in the summer, I thought we could plant a vegetable garden. Some kids in the area aren't getting enough fresh food to eat." The building excitement fizzled. "Now I don't have that kind of money."

"It's still a good idea." Jenna grew quiet, contemplative.

"Maybe if enough people come together, we can still make it work."

Bolstering her courage, she asked, "Would you like to come in for some coffee? These amazing treats need to be eaten." She held up the box of goodies.

She held her breath, waiting for a rejection.

"We'd love to," Grant put his hand on his wife's lower back and headed for her front door.

Excitement skipped though her veins as she raced up the stairs. This friendship thing might not be as hard as she thought. "Come on, Dempsey. Come on, boy."

The bulldog lumbered up the steps and inside like the obedient little dog he wasn't.

"Have you heard from Brad?" Jenna asked.

"No, and I don't expect to." At least that was the truth, but a change of subject was required.

She didn't want to talk about her brother or father or the dozens of other people in town who were arrested.

Grant squeezed his broad body into the tiny space between the kitchen table and the potbellied stove while Jenna settled on the other side of the small table by the counter. Both looked oversized in the small space.

"How's the bakery business?" Rachelle asked while she got out a set of mugs she found at a local garage sale. She avoided using the more formal china she hadn't been able to part with, and which had cost more per place setting than her monthly bills. Rent. Food. A lightbulb went on. Maybe she could sell the entire set! On eBay or something.

Now if she could only find a coffee pot. The small metal one that came with the cabin overflowed on the even days, and on the odd days it didn't work at all.

Jenna accepted the vintage creamer Rachelle handed her. "The shop is doing well since the ski slopes are staying open a bit longer this year."

The antique creamer had been her grandmother's, and looked out of place, but pouring cream from the carton still didn't settle quite right.

"It seems people are still managing to find their way into town," Rachelle dropped a couple of antique spoons on the small oak table, hoping no one would notice they were quality silver, and took a seat on the bed as the four walls started closing in, pressing her claustrophobia button.

Dempsey brushed against her leg and curled in a ball by her foot.

"Oh, that reminds me," Grant reached in his pocket to retrieve an envelope, "this came to my law office, but it's addressed to you."

Embarrassed heat brushed up Rachelle's cheeks as she reached for the envelope, then hesitated, unsure if she wanted to touch the thing. "I intended to do a change of address once I got a job and settled. For some reason, I thought the investigation and trial wouldn't take so long. The government still hasn't removed the hold on my personal investment accounts."

"Everything takes twice as long as you think it should."

So true. Then again, she'd held off listing an address with the postal service, because then she'd be obligated to update the Correctional Department in case her father wanted to contact her. The only plus of the tiny cabin was the shoebox didn't have a mailing address. The old Rachelle Clairemont didn't want to be found. Then again, neither did the new Rachelle.

"Aren't you going to open it?" Jenna leaned forward to look at the envelope.

"I already know what it is. My real estate license has been reinstated." She looked up to meet Grant's eyes. "Your father was our family attorney." She shrugged, "I put the law office as my temporary address thinking I would change the address once I got settled. At the time I didn't know where I would be living." *I certainly didn't think I'd still be living in Elkridge.*

"No worries. I'll let Peggy-Sue know to set your mail

aside. You can pick it up any time the office is open."

"They reinstated your license." Jenna scooted to the end of her chair. "That's wonderful news. Once you get your first property listed, I'll make some of those logo brownies you designed for an open house."

"That's nice of you, but I'll have to take a pass." She let out a long awkward breath. "Real estate was my dad's thing, and to be honest, it was something I just fell into. Besides, who would hire me? I can't imagine anyone in this town would entrust me with the sale of their home."

"There are a few people around," Grant suggested. "We could help with referrals."

"That's okay. I've got a few other ideas." She coaxed a smile into place as fear choked off her air.

She didn't have a clue where she could find a job, but one thing was sure. She wouldn't live the life her father demanded she live.

"How is the remodeling coming?" Grant asked with a curious glint in his eye. "I met the new owner in town today when he stopped for gas. Nice guy, even if a bit quiet."

Quiet. Jacob wasn't quiet. Not with her. "I suppose a game designer does lend itself to being an introvert, but he knows what he wants."

"So you've met him."

"This morning. I was just finishing up the work on his game room."

"Done. Already? Good for you."

For some reason Grant had always been kind to her, especially after his twin had decided to ski out of bounds and tangle with a tree a week before their wedding. Losing her fiancé was bad enough, but Jason had gone up to the Vail family cabin with another woman. The news outlets caught whiff of the jilted lover angle, and for weeks there was nowhere to hide.

Grant did his best to shield her from the vicious rumors, but the tabloid story took weeks before the harassment and innuendos and lies died down.

"How about some coffee?"

Jenna eyed the coffee pot, and the dribbled black liquid.

Rachelle chuckled over the do-I-have-to expression Jenna was doing her best to hide. "I don't blame you."

"Excuse me? Blame me for what?"

"Not wanting to drink that coffee."

"Oh. The coffee." Jenna tucked a strand of hair back into her braid. "It's a bit late in the day for coffee anyway. We're on our way to an early dinner, or late lunch, or whatever you want to call it. It's all-you-can-eat at More Than Meatballs. Why don't you join us?"

An invitation to dinner? Now that's something she never expected. "Thank you for the offer, but I've been gone most of the day. If I don't spend some time with Dempsey, he'll eat another pair of my shoes."

Jenna looked at Dempsey who wore an expression of utmost innocence. The little turd.

"You sure?" Grant leaned in, "because if you're afraid someone might say something—"

Rachelle waved him off. "I used to be, but I got over my fear weeks ago. It's part of the new me. I'm good." *Just keep refreshing your lip gloss, Rachelle, so no one can see past the shine.*

Jenna stood, and shoved her hands in her back pockets. "When I came to Elkridge, I was broke, hungry, and angry." She snorted out a chuckle. "I was sleeping in the park when Maggie found me. She dragged me over to the café, gave me a meal, and a job. Don't underestimate this town, Rachelle. There are some good people here who have a lot to give."

True, *but first I need to discover who I am, and how to be the person I always wanted to be.* "I appreciate you both for giving me a second chance. It means a great deal to me, but I don't want anyone to make this easy. My father hurt a lot of people, and I want to make amends."

"It doesn't mean you have to freeze to death. I brought some extra blankets in the Jeep because I know how cold this place can get at night."

"Blankets I will accept. And thank you," she took Jenna's hand, and managed to gracefully gag down another bite of humble pie, "and for talking Maggie into letting me stay here."

"There you go again." Jenna smiled with a wink. "Maggie's just thankful someone is living in the place. You staying here saves her from having to check on the place, or keep the water running to make sure the pipes don't freeze."

Grant held open the door, and stuck his foot out when Dempsey tried to make a run for it. Rachelle reached for the naughty dog.

"Still. I do appreciate the kindness," she said, stumbling over the words.

"Anytime," Jenna hurried down the steps, and waved.

She lifted her arm to respond as memories of the ruler marks, always applied above her shirt cuff to ensure no one at her school would ever see the bruises, made her pull inward.

Her first lesson about elitism came around the age of six, when her father beat words of gratitude out of her.

"Only the weak ask for help," he chastised. "The Clairemonts are above the rest," he declared.

She closed the door and set Dempsey on the hardwood floor, watching while he ran to get his favorite toy.

"Death is not the greatest loss in life. The greatest loss is what dies inside us while we live." She studied Dempsey, who was watching with his head tilted to the side, puzzling over what she was trying to say. "Do you know who said that? Norman Cousins. He was a professor, editor, and a pretty smart guy, but I'm not sure he was right."

She picked up Dempsey's stuffed cat, now missing

both eyes and an ear, and tossed the fuzzy thing to the farthest corner of the room. "The soul never dies. It just adapts."

Determination gripped her hard.

She would rise from the ashes and spread her wings, a phoenix with feathers of purple and blue and gold.

No one could stop her this time.

Chapter Four

Rachelle parked in front of the construction office trailer and pulled the visor down to check her makeup. She rubbed the corner of her mouth where her shaky hand had jerked outside the ruby red line. She was only meeting with Erik Sparks, after all, but he didn't know she was coming.

It was better this way.

She took a deep breath, gracefully exited the Mercedes, and tossed the purse straps over her shoulder.

"You don't know it yet, Erik Sparks, but you need my help." She rushed through a wardrobe check, then climbed up the steps to the twelve- by sixty-foot trailer.

Her former high school classmate sat slumped behind a makeshift desk. He hadn't changed much. A bit scruffy, with a day-old beard and a worn T-shirt to complete his signature look. She could barely see him past the desk piled with engineering drawings, paperwork, and files, but assumed a pair of baggy jeans rounded out his wardrobe. A cup with a week's worth of stains sat by his right hand. A half-eaten bagel by his left.

She closed her nostrils to the stench, which reminded her of gym clothes stuffed in a bag and forgotten. If she wasn't desperate, she might have left without a word.

"Hello, Sparky." She cranked up the friendly.

The construction owner peered at her over the top of his laptop. He blinked, then blinked again, his eyes squinting. "Rachelle? What are you doing here?"

She donned her game face, the one which said I-got-this, walked to the nearest chair, and took a seat on the front edge, trying to miss the dark smudge in the blue fabric. "How are you doing, Erik?"

His eyes narrowed further. "Fine. Why?"

She ran her hands down her legs to smooth the creases with her sweaty palms. "Rumor has it you have a new construction contract. Good for you." She should have put on more lip gloss to make smiling easier.

Erik rolled back in his office chair and crossed one ankle over the opposite knee. "You still haven't answered my question. What are you doing here, Rachelle?"

"Well..." she grabbed the edge of the chair to keep from fussing with her hair, "I need a job, and I bet you need an office manager. I ran my father's office for years, so I can run yours." She waved her hand like she was waving a wand. "All this mess on your desk will be organized and filed in no time, and I'll have your back office running like a well-oiled machine."

His stare could have been a laser beam, red and hot and focused. After a few seconds, his shoulders bounced with laughter. "I—" He pointed at her, his eyes watering. "I can't—"

He crossed his arms, wheezing and snorting until he could finally catch his breath...but his shoulders still bounced from the humor she failed to see.

"Rachelle Clairemont asking me for a job. Hell has seriously frozen over." He wiped his eyes with the inside of his shirtsleeve. "Why would you ever think I'd give you a job?"

Don't react. Stay calm. Rachelle gulped down her first response. She needed to think. She stifled the trembling distress. "I've managed several projects for my dad, if references are what you need."

"No. No. I don't need any references."

"But you do need office help. That's clear."

"You're probably right. And I'm sure you would do a good job, but you would be too much of a distraction."

She sat a little straighter. "If you're talking about us working together, I assure you it wouldn't be a problem."

His mouth hinted at a smile, but it was a mile away from reaching his eyes. "Oh, I know it wouldn't be a problem. You made it perfectly clear you didn't want anything to do with me when I asked you to prom. You know, you didn't need to make an ass of me in the lunchroom."

"I was making a point."

"And were you making a point when we attended the Fourth of July bonfire, and again when Grant Newhall set us up for a dinner date. I guess it took me a while to get the hint. Don't worry. I finally got your point."

"See..." she opened her eyes wider to stop his words from stinging, "...then there's no problem. I won't be a distraction."

"Oh, you'll be a distraction, all right. Each crew member will make an excuse to stop in here to get a whiff of your perfume."

She caught herself just before raising her wrist to her nose. She hadn't worn any perfume today. Not yesterday, either. What was his point?

Folding her hands in her lap, she concentrated on relaxing her muscles. "You might not understand, Erik. I've changed."

"Your circumstances have changed, for sure. You? I highly doubt it. Besides, I can't have a woman in the office. Too much drama."

"You know there are laws about diversity in the workplace," she offered the helpful advice, but the flash of dark anger made her gulp back any additional information she was about to share.

"Threatening people will not get you a job. I know the laws. In fact, one of my best foremen is a woman."

"Isn't that ironic." She lifted the brow she'd tweezed to perfection. "A foreman who's a woman."

Erik stood. "Now, there's the Rachelle I know. Sarcastic

and spiteful."

"Why, Erik, I didn't know you knew how to use such big words. Good for you for improving your vocabulary." She cringed, and held out her hand. "Erik, I shouldn't have—"

"Whatever you were going to say, don't. You'll just dig a deeper hole, and I'm already thinking about backing up one of my cement trucks to bury you. You should leave—now, before either of us says something we'll regret even more."

She should have ducked when he swung, but years of holding up her pride to take the blows head-on had become a habit. She would have to work harder at unraveling her father's psychological handiwork. Dejection settled in the pit of her stomach.

She nodded and stood. "Thank you, Erik, for at least hearing me out. Someday I hope you'll see things differently, and I hope you'll believe me when I say you're more than what people think of you."

"There you go again, being mean and speaking in riddles."

"I'm not being mean." She took a step forward, pressed the tips of her fingers into his desktop, and leaned in to look him in the eyes. "Just for the record, I never went out with you because you've always been in love with Connie Stillwater. You both love each other, but you," she pointed, "you've never felt you deserved her. The minister's daughter is sweet and kind and full of love, yet you've never felt good enough, so you went trotting after anything in a skirt, including me."

Erik leaned in, "You don't know squat."

"Oh, yeah? Then why is Connie's picture still the only one in your wallet?" His hand went to reach in his back pocket, then stalled.

Gotcha. She lifted her determined chin. He rolled forward to place his forearms on his desk.

"Why is it you women always like to play games and

try to change people?"

"I don't know the answer." A taste of honesty felt odd, but she swallowed the bittersweet flavor and kept going. "Maybe Connie was trying to change you because that's all she knew. Her father's in the business of making sinners see the light. Fathers can be pretty demanding of their daughters."

"Is that your excuse for being so mean? It's your father's fault?"

Shame heated her cheeks. "No. The way I acted in the past, I own. No one else." Rachelle took a step back and gathered her purse. "Thank you for your time, Erik. Good luck with your contract. I'll see you around."

"Don't count on it," he followed up a second before the office door swung shut with a bang.

Her heart dragged along with her feet. She held onto the railing on the way down the steps to make sure her legs would carry her upright and prevent a face-plant. Halfway to her car, she spotted the deputy patrol SUV sitting across the street.

Still on stakeout duty, huh, Deputy? She wouldn't be surprised if her phones were tapped, too.

She'd escaped, but her former life still had her shackled.

She tossed her purse into the passenger seat, started the car, navigated out of the parking lot, and came to a full stop at the corner just to make sure the deputy following her had no reason to pull her over. She made a quick stop at the hardware store, then headed home, all while dogged by the black SUV in the rearview mirror.

The car following her let her go when she turned onto the dirt road leading to her house.

"Finally." The tension in her shoulders eased. Thoughts of painting away the rest of the day eased a lightness into her heart.

Her mother had encouraged her creative dreams. Drawing. Painting. Photography. Sculpting. She tried them all and loved them all. If only she could make a living from her art.

She grabbed the handles of her shopping bags and made her way toward the house.

Halfway up the steps, she listened for Dempsey.

Nothing.

How odd.

He frequently growled or at least barked at her approach, but not this time.

She unlocked the door and twisted the handle. Seconds later, little white feathers floated around her feet and blew out the door.

Oh, noooo. You didn't.

She shifted the bags in her hand. "Dempsey, you little snot rag."

The counters. The table. The floor. Every inch was covered by down feathers. In the middle of her bed were the remnants of her favorite pillow, now shredded beyond repair.

"Dempsey!" she kicked the door shut and dropped the bags on the counter. "Get out here, now."

Little round eyes peered at her from beneath the bed.

"Come here." She softened her tone. "Come on."

Dempsey crawled from under the bed, his eyes watchful. She leaned to scoop him into her arms before he backed under the bed again.

She turned and sat on the bed, cradling him in her lap. "Did I ever tell you a dog bit me when I was five? I've always been afraid of dogs, so maybe that's why I've never learned how to take care of one. I'm not being a very good pet parent, am I? I leave you alone too much, and you get bored."

Dempsey stretched up to lick her chin, and she let him. "Thanks. I thought you would understand why it's taking me awhile to adjust to having a dog. I understand you're upset Brad left you, but it might make you feel better to know that ever since my mother left he's been unable to form attachments to people or pets. It's not your fault he left you behind."

The tears threatening all morning dribbled down her face. "He was always scared of our father. I tried to protect him the best I could."

She ran her hand over Dempsey's head and down his back, over and over again. "We both had so much anger and resentment we had to hide." She rubbed Dempsey's ear. "Erik was right. I was mean. I did things, said things, I've always regretted. Just like you. I bet you didn't mean to eat my pillow." She held Dempsey up and looked him in the eyes.

The dog looked away. "I bet you're mad because Brad just dumped you here and left. Abandoned you. He left me too, you know."

A tear plopped on her arm. She smeared the trickle of tears across her cheek. "We can't get stuck in what might have been. We need to adjust and keep moving forward. I'll have to remodel that house, even though destroying what I created will tear me apart. I'll do such an amazing job, Jacob Reyes will give me references. You'll see. And you'll learn a few things too, like how not to poop at the bottom of the front steps. I know you think it's funny when I step in it, but I don't."

She scratched Dempsey under the chin when he looked up. "If I can change, you can too. I'll make you a deal. If you start chewing on your chew toys and stop chomping on my stuff, I'll let you sleep on the bed. What do you think?"

Dempsey shifted in her arms, nuzzled a little closer, then tilted back his head.

"Deal?"

He barked, his look intent.

"Okay. We have a deal." She surveyed the room. "Now I need to clean up this mess, and design some rooms Mr. Reyes will like. Plus, we both need to eat."

Dempsey nuzzled his head into the crook of her arm.

"I know you want to play, but I don't have much time. I tell you what. I'll give you a good brushing. You like being brushed."

At hearing the word "brush" Dempsey wiggled out of her arms, then turned pinwheels on the floor.

The joy lasted for a few seconds before collapsing. She hung her head and gave in for a few seconds to the despair threatening to overwhelm her before pushing the sadness away.

She didn't have time to indulge.

She had a job to land.

Chapter Five

The sun hovered just above the mountaintop, turning the hillside purple. Across the sky a slow kaleidoscope unfolded in shades of purple, blue, orange and pink as twilight settled in.

Jacob set his wine glass on the deck railing and watched nature continue to paint her canvas.

He loved the sound of the ocean, but the mountains gave him a keener sense of peace. Elkridge reminded him of the Canadian Rockies and his childhood home. He missed his mom, her strength and her vulnerabilities. For years it was just the two of them against the world.

Nostalgia might have been why he picked this place. He sucked in a deep breath and, oddly enough, a perky blonde floated into his thoughts.

Rachelle reminded him of his mom—guarded, yet open. The contrast made him curious.

He didn't know much about her other than her work, but she projected an unmistakable inner strength, and her sturdy nature showed in the bold yet soft lines of her designs. The designs were simple, yet complicated. Comfortable, yet elegant. There was nothing out of place. Everything belonged. Yet the designs created a statement. That kind of design took talent, something that couldn't be taught. He didn't have the it-factor, and the lack of genius haunted him.

The instant Ben delivered her design boards, he knew the designer had a gift. The board brought his idea to life. The pencil sketch in the middle outlined the room, but the fabric and paint swatches and furniture elements pasted around the edges gave the room texture. The design was well-thought-out and simply spectacular.

He appreciated artists who could take an idea and turn the theory into such a perfectly targeted reality. A rare quality indeed.

"Jacob?"

The rich, feminine voice calling from the pathway leading to the back deck captured his attention. He leaned over the deck railing but didn't see anyone.

The vibration of footsteps made him turn toward the stairs leading to the yard.

"Hey." Rachelle emerged from below like the morning sun rising over the mountains.

"Hey." Her simple smile elicited one from him. "Why didn't you come in the front?"

She gestured over her shoulder. "No one answered the door." Concern tinged her voice, and her brows dipped lower over her intelligent eyes. "Is this still a good time to work on your chairs?"

She'd dressed casually in kick-back jeans with a white blowsy shirt tucked into the front, and a floral sweater coat that hung just above her knees. Today her hair was down and fell in curls to just below her shoulders. Her rich yet relaxed style was her own, but she'd fit on the cover of any shabby chic magazine without a doubt.

After a few seconds, he remembered to breathe. "I must have been distracted. I've gotten used to Ben reminding me of the time." He angled in to get a full whiff of her floral scent. "And don't worry about the chairs. I finished putting them together this morning."

"That was my job." If her arms hadn't been full, he suspected she might have crossed them and given him what-for.

"Yes...well...Ben needed to leave for San Diego this morning, and I wanted to test some new programming."

"Is everything okay?"

He liked the way her concern was instant, then aloof.

"With the game? Sure. With Ben, who knows? I sponsor a charity event each year for kids whose parents are terminally ill. We're having some challenges with the venue which require Ben's problem-solving abilities."

She nodded slowly. "I saw the pictures of last year's event on your website. The video of your mother was a nice touch."

The bittersweet memories of compiling the pictures and old family videos warmed his core. "Someone's been doing their homework."

A smile flickered across her mouth, then slowly disappeared. "It's easier for me to create a design if I know the person."

Interesting. He lifted his glass of wine to take a sip. "Yet I know nothing about you. I don't even know your last name. Ben always just called you Rachelle the Remarkable."

Surprise darted across her eyes before she wiped her expression slate clean, as if she was afraid to show any emotions at all. She walked to the other side of the deck table to set her purse and portfolio down. Eventually, her gaze met his. "My name is Rachelle Clairemont."

The way she said her name, almost like an apology, gave him pause.

Clairemont? Clairemont? Hmmm. The name sounded familiar. Why did he know that name?

Slowly the memory file drawers opened. The conversations with his lawyers. The signing of real estate closing papers. He studied her, then the house behind her.

He braced against the blast of guilt. "This was *your* home."

"Yes." The crisp, clear response left no room for doubt. She lifted her chin a little higher. "It's the reason I hesitated to accept your offer. If you want to withdraw your design proposition, I'll understand, but I've had second thoughts. I believe I can give you what you want."

Her hands gave away her stress. With each passing second, her fingers whitened with escalating tension.

"Ben never questioned the association," she said, "and I never had the opportunity to reveal the connection."

The lifelong thread of vigilant protectiveness that was his nature stitched up his spine. "Withdraw my offer? I don't think so. I meant it when I said your designs are amazing." He approached her slowly, searching, waiting for her to tell him how to proceed. "I'm more concerned about you. If you would prefer not to take the job, I'd fully understand."

A hesitant smile formed, the first genuine sign of happiness he'd seen from her. "I can do the job. In fact I've jotted down a few ideas." She reached for her leather portfolio and slid out some picture boards similar to the entertainment room design. "I spent some time today creating samples for you to look at."

What she called samples were handcrafted boards filled with paints, fabrics, and in some places wood samples.

Wow. "You created these today?"

She picked up one of the boards. "Yes. Here's an idea for the master bedroom. I like this one the best."

The charcoal grays, with silver and cream accents scattered around a master bed, could only have come out of his head. How did she do it?

"Here's the design for the closet," she handed him another board.

Black shelving to hold suits, jackets, pants, shirts, and shoes lined three walls. In the center there was a tie butler, and even a case to house his watch collection. He glanced at his Rolex, then her.

"How did you know I like watches?"

She shrugged. "In the images I found, you were wearing a different watch in every picture. I did a little research and discovered some of the watches you wear need to be worn or rocked." She pointed at the watch drawer again. "There's a mechanism in this drawer to simulate body movement to keep the watches wound. And see this feature here?" She pointed at a metal door. "Press a button and a metal door will slide in place to keep your valuables safe. Elkridge is a pretty safe place to live, but I don't think you want to take the chance of having your precious items stolen."

He leaned in. "Is there anything you haven't thought of?"

"I bet you'll let me know if I've missed something." Her eyes flashed with a hint of humor.

For a long moment, he couldn't say anything. He lingered to breathe in her springtime freshness. "Are you hungry? I promised you pizza, and Ben prepared the food before he left. All I have to do is toss the pizza into the oven."

Her violet eyes turned a lighter shade of purple, mirth dancing in her eyes. "Not a cook, I take it."

"Put it this way, if it isn't eggs, cereal, or pancakes, you wouldn't want to eat it."

"Got any beer?"

"A beer I can manage. Ben loves trying new beers, and filled the entire beverage fridge with an assortment of local beers. You can take your pick."

"Men are all alike."

The generalization made his neck muscles tighten.

She took a step back, bit her lip, then her face went blank again. She didn't retract the statement, only picked up her bags and designs and relocated to the kitchen, stopping at the beverage fridge she obviously had built into the kitchen island.

"Not all men are alike." He set his wine glass on the massive granite countertop, letting the irritation her words caused slink away. "I'd like to think I'm a bit different."

"Men with money and power would like to think they

are unique, different. But from what I've seen, the common traits outweigh those that are distinct."

He didn't like the way the conversation had turned. Her aloof nature protected more than just her privacy. "Who hurt you, Rachelle?"

He waited with every sense alert for her to continue. Waited for the shape of her mouth to change, and her eyes to shutter. She gave nothing away.

"Let me rephrase." He paused to select the correct wording. "I've been remiss in getting to know you, and I like to know the people I work with, especially if they will be in my home."

Her arms crossed, tightened into a defensive barrier. "Let's just say my life hasn't been easy. Most of my life I've had to deal with powerful men. I had to learn to adapt. To survive. Men with money and power make me leery," she said, in a way that made each word count.

"Good."

"Good?" she choked, and her eyes opened wider.

"Yes. You should be careful about the people you allow into your life. You deserve to live life the way you want, Rachelle. Don't let anyone or anything stand in your way."

For a long moment she didn't say anything. Just stared. Then her eyes narrowed. "Seems to me you've been hurt yourself."

"I was fourteen when my mom died of kidney failure. After that, my life wasn't my own anymore—at least not until I got out of college. The only thing my father cared about was good grades. Once I got my first job, I made a commitment to live the life I want to live. A life of my choosing."

Although recently he'd realized his efforts had gone toward getting his father's attention and proving he was more than a photo his father showed his colleagues.

What a waste of time and effort.

He needed to focus on building a new video game,

something he could be proud of, and forget about what his father wanted. Yet no new ideas were solidifying.

His creative well had run dry.

A lonely desolation made his skin crawl. He leaned in, craving comfort, and was stopped by her palm on his chest.

"Mr. Reyes, I believe we need to amend our working proposal to make sure we stay on the same page."

He immediately took a step back, and lifted his wine glass, taking a deep swallow to douse a need he hadn't felt in a very long time. "And what do you propose?"

"I've worked with a lot of men in the past. Most of them make assumptions—the wrong assumptions." She returned his intensity. "I'll work with you on your interior design, but I want your promise. No flirting. No innuendos. No kisses. And certainly no sex."

"Agreed," he said without taking a breath. "Anything else?"

And just like that, the world tipped back onto its axis.

For some odd reason, she believed him.

How could she not?

The raw sincerity in his eyes, voice, and body language matched the statement. Over the years she'd gotten pretty good at observing how people reacted rather than what they said, and she'd bet he was telling the truth.

"That's good," her hand dropped to her side. "Really good."

"For who? Me? You?" He shook his head. "I don't think so." He reached out a hand then his fingers folded back into his palm.

His need to touch her was written clearly in block letters across his hand. His resistance, though, was darnright sexy. The demonstrated respect sent a thousand glittering chills down her spine.

"Damn, you are so tempting, but I won't go back on my word." He shoved his hands into his pockets. "I know you don't believe me, but you'll see I'm a man of my word." He leaned in. "But if I'm not mistaken, I believe you feel the connection we share. I felt it the first time I set eyes on you. We connect. The connection shows in every detail of what you created for me."

Resentment over his bold assumptions rolled up from her core like a wildfire through dry grass. But she couldn't deny what she felt when she gazed into his sexy brown eyes. "Do all men get a master's degree in arrogance?"

"Don't mistake arrogance for confidence. One day, if or when you acknowledge the attraction, I leave it to you to decide the next steps."

"You seem sure of yourself."

"Men can be pricks, Rachelle," his gaze darkened, and intensified, "but I'm not one of them. Never have been. My mother might have been a single mom, but she raised me right. However, it doesn't mean you don't deserve my honesty."

"Honesty?" She moved closer, still sensing no danger. "Time will tell. Men have carnal instincts. Some more than others."

"Since you've studied me, you know I don't date much. There are very few people I allow into my life. You're an extraordinary woman, Rachelle. Smart. Talented. I find you very attractive. Who wouldn't?" He scanned her face. He pulled his hands from his pockets and drummed his fingers against his thigh while he debated. "While you're in my home, you will be treated with respect. You will see there's a difference between me and those assholes from your past who should have their noses readjusted."

She studied him closely. There it was again. His honesty. She could see the truth in his eyes. "At least you realize there's a difference."

"Rachelle, at some point there will be a man in your

life you can trust—probably more than one. Maybe I'll be the first." His eyes had softened, and he lifted his hand, palm outstretched, offering her hope. "So are you in or out?"

She stared at the long fingers on his broad hand. Her eyes traced the lines on his palm. And just like that, she placed her hand in his. She wanted...no, needed...to connect with someone. During the last several weeks loneliness left her parched and aching for human connection. His skin was warm, soothing.

"In," she whispered, hating the weakness in her voice. Her eyes stung from the emotional release. "It takes me a while to trust people."

"And initially you push people away to protect yourself. I get it."

She turned his palm over to trace his long lifeline, then withdrew. "There haven't been many people in my life I could trust."

His eyes gentled. "I'm sorry."

"For?"

"It's a sad way to live...and because the money in my bank account scares you. I can assure you I have never used money to make someone do something they didn't want to do."

"To your point, money doesn't scare me. It's the people behind the money, that's who I'm leery of." Admitting the fear sent hot flashes pulsing up her neck and cheeks.

He laid a hand gently over hers. "I do have money— more than most—but underneath it all, I'm just a guy who likes to play video games and help kids who don't understand they will be okay even after their parent dies."

He opened himself up, exposed himself on purpose to generate an environment of security. She accepted his gift for what it was, and let the cool Colorado night breeze coming through the sliding glass encircle them and hold the two hurt souls safe.

A leisurely smile stretched across his face, like a cat waking up from a nap.

"Ready to indulge in some carbs?"

She searched his face, daring to hope a person could be in her life without wanting to control her, or bend her to his will. She wanted a man who could see her as a partner, not some woman to be put in her place.

She ran her thumb over his hand the way he did hers. "Do you know how to turn on the oven?"

A robust laugh came bouncing out and made her smile. "That's a valid question. How about you teach me how it's done? I don't want to starve until Ben returns."

"You might need to learn how to cook. There aren't many places around here for takeout."

She could have sworn he leaned in a little closer, but when she double-checked, he hadn't moved. He was keeping his promise, but the look in his eyes also promised her he wouldn't make resisting him easy.

"After we get the pizzas in the oven, I'd like to look at those design boards again."

"So you like the designs?"

"No. I don't like them, I love them. Normally I go through dozens of designs before I find one I can live with. You get me. And the designs are spot on. Now if I could only teach my game designers to read my mind, I'd be set."

"Sounds like you're frustrated because they can't translate your ideas," she suggested after reading the agitation on his face.

"For the past five years we've had meeting after meeting until someone finally comes up with something we can use. Not getting it right the first time takes time and money, and when the game's already been pitched to launch at a certain time, it adds a great deal of pressure."

"I thought you sold your game."

"Yes, but I have investors who want to invest in my next game. If I don't come up with a new world soon, they'll invest somewhere else."

"Ah. Got it."

She showed him how to work the oven, then slid onto the stool at the kitchen island to avoid taking over. "When I was in high school, I came up with a game design. In my head, I laid out this whole city filled with magical beings. There were mountains and rivers. I even threw in a forest filled with odd creatures."

He slid the pizza into the oven, then reached for some dishes. "Do you play?"

Between the excitement in his voice and the way his entire body almost wiggled like a wagging puppy, his delight was palpable. It was almost like watching her brother get his first baseball bat. She didn't want to squash his enthusiasm, but had to correct the assumption. "I don't, but my brother does." *Or he did.* "After watching him play for hours, I came up with this idea for an alternative world where everything was beautiful, yet corrosive. "

He searched her face, thinking. "Interesting choice of words. Was your city big or small?"

"When I design, I always start small and work my way out, it's easier than getting overwhelmed in the details."

"But how do you know your design fits in the wider picture?"

"When I design a room, I think of the basics. How a person will naturally navigate a room, the lighting, both simulated and natural, and where furniture will naturally fall. After that I add color and texture. From room to room the change is gradual, soothing." She shrugged. "For what you're building, I would think you'd want to do the exact opposite. You're building utopia in a dysfunctional way. Things will appear normal, then warp into something different—unexpected—to catch the players' attention."

"Yes, but what does that utopia look like? That's my problem."

"I created a world made of crystals. With each refraction of light, the world and the characters inside change. One minute the character is beautiful, the next a demon, or fairy or warlock. My characters don't shift, like a shape-shifter, but transform based on how powerful the gamer has become. The more powerful, the more the player can see the true essence of the character. In the beginning, the gamer wouldn't know who to trust, but as the game progresses, more and more is revealed."

"I love it." He tapped his fingers on the countertop. "Utopia meets dystopia in a whole new, multi-level way."

She laughed at his exuberant expression. The sensation felt strange. Her life hadn't been fun. And the last time someone made her laugh was so long ago she couldn't pinpoint the moment.

She picked up the pile of mail on the counter to straighten the stack. "My characters are rooted in mythology and lore, only because I've always thought the old designs are cool. I wonder. What do you think would happen if the gods ruled in a technologically advanced society? Would technology find a way to nullify their superpowers? Would the gods figure out how to dismantle the artificial intelligence superstructure?"

He tapped a couple of fingers on his head. "A fight for power in utopia, where greed and domination shouldn't exist." He folded his arms, his hand cupping his jawline, squeezing and releasing. "The characters would have to reflect the world."

"That's the easy part. In one of my art classes our assignment was to take two forms and combine them. Like a tree and flower, or a light bulb and lamp. I combined a cat and a dog. It wouldn't be too hard to place a mythological god in a futuristic setting."

The way he smiled at her made her toes curl. *Oh, man.* He could make her want things she shouldn't ever want.

"Rachelle?"

A Fourth of July sparkler sizzle sent tingles every

which way. She should accuse him of reading *her* mind, the way he was looking at her. Could he know the sensual images swarming her brain? "Yes, Jacob?"

"You still want to stick to our agreement?"

This wasn't good. Not good at all. Her brain said yes while her head voted a firm—very firm— no. His eyes narrowed, and he took a couple of steps, and rounded the edge of the counter. He lifted her hand from her lap.

"I thought you agreed," she studied his eyes.

"I did agree, but I specifically said I wouldn't make it easy for you."

"Jacob...I..."

"Tell me you want me...want this."

No. No I don't. No. No. No. But she couldn't say a word. His mouth hovered a half an inch from hers, and she wanted to feel his skin against hers.

"Tell me what you want. It's your choice."

"I..."

"Bro, my man!" An unfamiliar voice yelled from the hallway. "What's up?

Jacob jerked back. "Larson. What are you doing here?"

Chapter Six

Larson stood in the doorway with one arm around a redhead, the other around a blonde. A brunette in shorts covering not much stood nearby. His fake Cheshire cat grin was telling, and sent a swarm of uneasiness crawling across Jacob's skin.

"I decided you need some company." Larson released the women and spun around in a circle, looking at the vaulted ceiling and then out the massive windows looking across to the mountain ridge. "What a great pad." He tipped his head back and staggered a few steps, then leaned forward, squinting. "Is that a silver cow's skull on the wall?"

Jacob's stomach clutched.

His business partner was feeling no pain. Feeling no guilt for having broken the promise he made less than twenty-four hours earlier to stay sober and off drugs. Jacob wasn't sure he could go through the anguish of watching Larson hit bottom again.

Jacob stepped in front of Rachelle. "Larson. I thought you were in California."

"I wanted to party. Have some fun."

Larson put an arm around Jacob's shoulders, and the stench of cigarettes and booze triggered his gag reflex. Sliding out from under his best friend's arm, he demanded, "Dude. What are you doing? You've been down this road before, and it doesn't end well."

"I booked us some rooms." Larson patted Jacob's shoulder.

LYZ KELLEY / 53

"I've got work to do. The investors are expecting a proposal on their desk by Thursday. You were supposed to be investigating the software we talked about and setting up a new development environment."

Larson waved him off. "Work. Work. Work. All you do is work. You gotta have some fun, buddy."

One of the girls giggled and flopped down on the great room's couch. She wasn't in any better shape.

Larson squinted, then tromped to the counter to pick up one of Rachelle's design plates. He spun the board across the counter like he was throwing away a piece of trash. "What's this?" He pointed.

"Just some ideas for my master bedroom." Jacob stepped in between Larson and Rachelle. "Take it easy, buddy."

"Don't let her design anything else." Larson poked Jacob's chest with every word. "I'm the designer. Me. Not some big-boobed bobblehead." He reached past Jacob's shoulder toward Rachelle, but Jacob managed to hold him back despite the height difference.

"I should go." Rachelle already had her purse over her shoulder, and was scooting out of reach.

Damn it.

She looked at him with such understanding he wanted to punch Larson. He didn't want her to understand anything. This wasn't how life was supposed to be. He wanted his smart, funny, dependable, study-buddy back.

Jacob nodded. "It's probably for the best."

"Yeah. Run away, little girl." Larson flicked his wrist, shooing her away.

"Will you get back to me on the designs?" Rachelle asked, ignoring Larson.

The only thing he could do was nod. When she turned to leave, he felt like a helpless idiot, but there was nothing he could say to make a better impression.

"Hey! You. Blondie," Larson called after her. "Remember, I make the designs."

She didn't acknowledge the slurred words. She just kept walking, and Jacob didn't blame her. At least she didn't race out of the house.

Jacob held out his hand. "Give them to me."

Larson shriveled inward, and walked around him, ignoring Jacob's demand. "Let's go have some fun." Larson pointed toward the front door. "Our limo's outside."

Jacob walked to the front picture window. Sure enough, there was a man in a black suit leaning up against a stretch limo taking a smoke break.

A burdened breath released in a fluid rush as he let his hands fall to his sides. "Tell you what. Why don't I arrange for the driver to take these lovely ladies back to the airport so you and I can talk." *And I'll get you sobered up.*

"Stop worrying. I've got everything under control."

Jacob lifted Larson's arm and searched his pockets.

"Hey." Larson tried pushing him away. "What are you doing? Stop touching me."

Jacob lifted a prescription bottle of pain meds from Larson's front pocket. "Where did you get these?"

"I hurt my back."

Jacob stepped closer, looking directly into Larson's eyes. "When?"

Larson studied a spot on the ceiling that most likely wasn't there, then reached to scratch his shoulder, a tell-tale sign Larson was trying to buy time to come up with another lie.

But he couldn't lie.

Jacob and his buddy had spent the past ten years together. Jacob had been covering for him—he even got arrested a couple of times so Larson could avoid a probation violation. But now his patience was wearing thin.

"Tell you what." He pocketed the pills. "Why don't you go upstairs, check out the place? And I'll entertain these ladies for a few minutes."

"I know what you're trying to do, man. Be cool." Larson accused, sticking out his lower lip like a five-year-old.

Jacob got even closer. "Is that what you using is about? Being cool? Belonging?"

Larson stumbled backward and blinked. When Larson paled, Jacob grabbed his arm and snatched back the design boards, but Larson yanked away, knocking himself off-balance and careening to the floor. He sat wide-eyed for a moment, then started laughing—the way a person laughs when they have nothing to laugh about.

Larson rolled onto his knees, and the redhead grabbed an elbow to help him stand, but the first effort failed.

Jacob stepped in front of the struggling pair. "Why don't I help you upstairs so you can sleep for awhile?"

Larson struggled to his feet and eventually made it vertical. He waved a hand in front of his face. "I smell smoke."

Smoke?

Crap.

Jacob rushed to the kitchen, shoved his hand into the silicon mitt, and opened the oven door. Sure enough, both pizzas were singed black. Smoke billowed out of the oven, and he looked at the ceiling, hoping the smoke detectors wouldn't go off, but his hope was smashed a second later by the blaring horns.

Shit. Shit. Shit. That's all he needed was a visit from the fire department.

He punched the oven off, grabbed a dishcloth, and furiously waved the small cotton square at the ceiling. After a few dozen waves the blasted blaring stopped. He grabbed the charcoal rounds, and shoved the pans and burned pizzas into the sink, then turned on the water.

The sound of a car's engine starting and pulling out of the drive added another heaping layer of frustration to the mix.

He grabbed his phone and dialed Larson, then disconnected when the phone went to voicemail. He scrolled to his friend-finder app, but Larson had blocked him, so he shot off a text to Larson's sister and Courtney to let them both know what had happened.

Damn you, Larson.

Jacob leaned against the counter, hanging his head. Frustration stifled his breath.

God, how he wished he'd never made the deal to sell his company. If he hadn't, Larson wouldn't have had access to wads of cash, or the time to get into trouble.

Fear tightened his throat. If Larson didn't get his act together, he'd be dead, and it would be Jacob's fault.

Jacob grabbed his rental car keys and headed for the door. Maybe Larson would have the driver stop in the little town for some snacks. It would only take a few minutes to check. Hiding a limo in a town the size of Elkridge wouldn't be easy.

He made his way down the hill and took a right onto Bridge Street, then a left on Main. He searched left and right, then turned on Ash. Nothing. He tapped his fingers on the steering wheel. When he got to the end of Ash, he turned into the parking lot of More Than Meatballs.

His dinner was burned. And far worse, in less than a month his life had skidded completely out of control.

Right now should have been the happiest time of his life.

He'd achieved success.

He had more money in the bank than he ever imagined possible.

Yet his success had brought with it an unexpected outcome.

The layer of gloom burdened his heart.

He entered the restaurant and debated whether to take out or dine in. Echoes of his lonely, empty existence made him reexamine his need to eat alone. He requested a table and followed the hostess to a booth.

He sent Larson another text and waited while the waitress brought him the requested glass of Chianti.

He thumbed through some emails, then dropped his phone on the table to let his mind settle.

Man, I'm tired.

The thought barely finished when a shadow fell across the table. "Mind if I join you?"

A tall man with a half-serious, half-friendly face hovered next to his elbow. His taupe pants and blue shirt with a sheriff's badge attached to his shirt pocket couldn't be a good sign. Neither could the intent look. The sheriff was definitely on duty.

Had Larson done something stupid? One of the women? Both were possible. "Help yourself," Jacob nodded toward the other side of the booth.

He had nothing to hide. Though back when he was fifteen, he might have had reason to make a run for it.

He'd hated being relocated to a new city. Cutting class, hanging out with the wrong crowd, and bending every rule he guaranteed he was on a first-name basis with the local cops. But in college, he realized he wasn't just pissing his dad off, he was hurting himself and sabotaging his future.

The sheriff slid into the booth and set his hat on the table. "Mr. Reyes, I'd like to introduce myself. I'm Joe Gaccione. I understand you bought the old Clairemont place."

"Is there a problem?" he asked, trying to read the man's intentions.

"I'm not sure." He rested a forearm on the table. "A couple of months ago the FBI and DEA were here making several arrests. The town's been pretty shaken up." Joe paused but his eyes still gathered data. "A few hours ago, a limousine hit town and headed up to your place."

Ah, so?

Jacob took a sip of his wine, letting the taste of cherry and plum swirl in his mouth before swallowing. "I can assure you, Sheriff, it's not my intention to cause any trouble." *In fact, I'm looking for some peace and quiet.*

"Good to hear, because I got a call saying there was a limousine full of people who were being disorderly."

Jacob closed his eyes, working hard to avoid the anger from spilling over. "That would be my business partner," *possibly my former partner if he doesn't straighten up.* "I'm sure it's the meds he's taking for a back injury, but..." No. This time there would be no more buts. He wouldn't make excuses for Larson anymore.

"Reports say your buddy's certainly feeling no pain. At least he wasn't driving."

The drug abuse therapist warned Jacob to have patience, give Larson support and understanding without trying to be co-dependent and take responsibility for Larson's actions. Yet how could he support Larson? Then again, how could he stand by Larson if he was intent on destroying his life?

"At least he wasn't driving," Jacob concurred.

"Drug addicts are not welcome in Elkridge. And if the dozens of arrests didn't send a clear message, I'm not sure what will. I'm doing my best to keep this town clean."

Dozens of arrests? Wow. The stern warning came through loud and clear. "It's a worthy fight, Sheriff, and one I appreciate you taking on." If only every city would take up the same fight, yet in some places getting drugs was as easy as getting a gumball out of a candy machine.

"Thank you for saying so. Drugs took the life of my brother."

"Did he overdose?"

"No, a drug trafficker named Richard Clairemont murdered him. Have you ever heard the name?"

Criminy. "Is Rachelle Clairemont his daughter?"

"Yes, she is." Joe leaned on his forearms. "Did she have anything to do with your business partner's visit?" The way Joe laid out the question seemed he was more curious than accusatory. Yet he kept his eyes even and casual. Jacob got the impression the simple question had a few complexities below the surface.

He matched the sheriff's posture. "She doesn't even know Larson. Why are you asking?"

"You must have read the news."

Jacob's hand-tapping stilled, and he flattened his palms on the table. "Actually, I find most news reporting outlets biased these days. If I want to know something, I ask one of my assistants to do the research rather than waste my time with colored commentary."

"Maybe you should take a peek now and then." Joe scratched behind his ear.

"If there's a problem, Sheriff, I need to know. I've employed Ms. Clairemont to redecorate my home. My gut says I can trust her. Are you telling me I have another problem I need to deal with?"

"No. No problem. I guess everyone deserves a second chance—and that includes Rachelle. She's been through a lot."

"Like?"

"Can't say. That's for Rachelle to tell, not me."

His respect for the sheriff grew. "Would you know where I could find her? I've tried to call, but I just get an answering machine. I want to make sure she's okay. My friend may have scared her."

"Scared her? I doubt it. If what she's been through didn't scare her, I doubt anything you toss her way will." Joe crossed his arms. "But you seem like a decent enough guy." He pointed east. "If you head out of town, just past the café, you'll see a turnoff to the left. Follow the road, and you'll come to a couple of cabins. Take the fork to the left, and you should see her blue Mercedes if she's home."

Joe slid out of the booth and waved Jacob off as he began to stand. Jacob held out his hand instead. "Thanks for the introduction, Sheriff. I appreciate what you're doing to keep this town clean."

Joe nodded. "You need anything, anything at all, just reach out."

A few seconds later, Jacob's meal arrived, but he was no longer hungry. All he wanted to do was find a little cabin in the woods with a golden-haired beauty inside.

"Goldilocks." He chuckled and wondered if she might be living with three bears.

But he doubted it, since it didn't seem her life had been a fairy tale.

When he arrived in Colorado he expected to find peace and quiet. Time to work. Dream about his new game. But so far there'd been nothing but unrest.

He hadn't slept well.

This morning he'd meditated and breezed through every turning point in his life. An epiphany struck. Under the surface, his father's lack of parental affection and dismissal of his talents had poked and prodded and pushed him to be a success.

He hadn't forced his parents to get married just because the pregnancy stick turned blue. Nor had he asked the judge to force his father to step up and take responsibility.

Just the opposite.

At least his early success hadn't derailed him as it had Larson.

He didn't have all the answers, but one thing was certain—he wanted to find out what happened to Rachelle Clairemont.

Whatever it was, it couldn't have been good.

Chapter Seven

Jacob walked up the warped steps and turned to study the rutted dirt drive.

Yep, there was her car. But why was the stylish, competent woman he met, the woman who once lived in a house the size of a small castle, now living in a cabin smaller than his garage? Certainly her father's crimes had nothing to do with her.

He lifted his hand to knock, then hesitated.

Rachelle opened the cabin door and tugged the edges of her knit sweater tight across her chest. "Jacob, what are you doing here?" She stuck out her foot to keep her French bulldog from dashing out of the cabin.

He again searched the cabin's open yard, then turned back to look in her eyes. "I came to apologize."

"For?" Her eyebrows popped up. "You didn't do anything wrong," she added softly. "Your friend is messing up. Not you."

Yet he was closer to Larson than anyone else in his buddy's life, and he still couldn't get him to listen. He didn't like to fail—and he was failing his friend. He squeezed the back of his neck to ease the building pain. "Rachelle, I..."

She tightened her grip on the door handle, and glanced over her shoulder, clearly uncomfortable. The worry in her eyes gave him a punch to the gut. "I should go. I just wanted to make sure you're okay."

"I would offer you some coffee, but the coffee maker and I don't seem to get along very well." She bit her lip.

"But I have a couple bottles of wine I've been saving. Seems like today might be the right time to open one of them."

He eased closer. "I'd like that." Remembering he had a to-go bag in his hand, he lifted his arm. "Since Larson ruined your dinner, I brought some penne pasta and some chicken parmesan."

She reached for the bags and held them up to the fading sunlight. "I see you found More Than Meatballs. It's said Mrs. Gaccione's Bolognese is the best around."

Gaccione, as in Joe Gaccione, one and the same. He'd missed the connection. That wasn't the only connection he'd apparently missed.

The town was even smaller than he thought. "You've never eaten there?"

Her face flushed. "No. I never had the opportunity."

Strange. "Then I guess we'll give the meatballs a try together."

He brushed by her, close enough to get a whiff of her lush, fresh, floral scent. The sweet undertones with a bold musk overlay matched her perfectly.

She set the bags on the counter and retrieved a couple of baroque-style fine china plates befitting any formal dining room. Next she retrieved a couple of crystal glasses, classy-looking enough to be hand cut, from another cupboard. The ornate flatware set next to the plates gleamed like only sterling silver could.

"Rachelle?"

She kept her back turned and gripped the counter like a lifeline.

"The sheriff stopped me in town. He told me your father murdered his brother. I suppose I could find out what happened on the internet, but I'd rather hear it from you. Would you mind telling me what happened?"

Very slowly she turned to face him, her beautiful face devoid of color. Tears pooled in her eyes, and she struggled for a breath.

"I..." She slumped into the chair like a rag doll.

Like a moron, he sat there and did nothing, for a second, then swept her into his arms. He held on while the wall she had built to keep the rest of the world out cracked, then shattered into a million pieces.

"Shhh. It's okay." He ran a hand up and down her back to soothe away the hurt.

Her body vibrated with the suffering. She clung to him with everything she had.

When her shuddering sobs eased, he loosened his grip. "Hey, where's that take-no-prisoners woman I met the other day?"

She swiped fingertips under her eyes. "You're right." She stood, straightened her sweater, and patted her hair.

He tore a section off the paper towel roll sitting on the counter and handed her the sheet.

"Thanks."

He leaned sideways to look at her face. "There's this character in my video game called Adira Cato. She's strong and wise, and she can pretty much kick anybody's ass. You remind me of her."

"I bet she doesn't cry."

"Only because the designers haven't been able to figure out how to simulate tears."

A weary smile limped into place. "Does she get to wear a cool set of armor?"

"Of course. And she can morph into a metal lioness and leap from building to building. It's pretty cool."

She nodded slowly. "But she's not real."

"No, but you are."

She sucked in a quiet breath, and he liked the reaction. More than anything, he wanted her to believe he could take her breath away.

Rachelle couldn't believe she just slimed a guy she

barely knew with a hard, ugly cry. She felt better, but only just.

She looked around the room, repelled by what she saw.

She'd worked hard every day, learning, planning, executing—and for what? To live in a room smaller than her walk-in closet through no fault of her own? Although the no-fault bit wasn't exactly true.

She should have found a way to escape her father long ago. But fear had always been a big part of why she never left. If she had run, she'd always live in fear of being found. Her father became more and more violent as the years progressed. Staying with him was safer than rebelling.

Jacob shouldn't feel sorry for her.

Her father had twisted her into a monstrous person, a person she didn't even recognize, was ashamed to recognize. Erik was right. She was mean to a lot of people, her way of dealing with the anger she had no idea how to control.

Now her goal was to find a way to help the town heal. She hadn't done a very good job yet, but she was determined to keep trying.

"For what it's worth, I have a friend who went through detox in Arizona last year." She pulled on a long strand of hair, twisting and pulling the strands in a circle. "The place wasn't cheap, but Tiffany's been clean for a while now, and the place offers lifetime support, 24/7."

"How did you get her to check herself in?"

She smoothed her hair back into place, then caught herself and left it a bit messy. "I didn't, actually. There's a baker here in town. She owns Dreamy Delights. You should stop in sometime." Rachelle reached for some serving spoons. "Tiffany ran into Jenna one night at a restaurant." Rachelle let the retold story unfold in her mind. "Tiffany doesn't normally listen to anyone, but Tiffany said Jenna, a stranger at the time, told her exactly what she needed to hear."

"And that was?"

"I'm not exactly sure, something about using drugs and not liking herself and deserving a better life."

"That sounds like good advice." Jacob gave her a soft assessment. "And what do you deserve, Rachelle?"

Without even thinking, the little voice in her head said *you don't deserve anything*, but before the thought finished she squashed it. She'd done nothing to deserve the life she lived, but she wasn't about to throw herself a pity party.

A couple of weeks ago she had burned all the photographs of the past in her small, potbellied stove. She didn't want that girl to exist any longer. She burned her old life into tiny flakes of nothing but gray powder. She wanted to take new pictures. Create new memories.

"If I'm honest, I don't know what I deserve. I'm still trying to figure out my life. What I do know is I'll never again be someone's puppet. I did what I needed to survive. But I don't just want to survive anymore. I want to find my own way."

He hesitated, then leaned closer. "Will you tell me what happened?"

Her eyes flicked away, then slowly swung back towards him. "I don't know the details, and that's the truth."

He held out his hands. "I'm not here to judge."

"I know." She shoved away from the counter and slipped into the chair. "My father was always a hard man to live with, and he got more controlling and demanding after my mother left us when I was five and my brother almost three. He was enraged that she'd left him. My life was never the same after that. In a way he groomed me to take my mother's place. I was to be entertaining, intelligent, sociable, yet an elitist. He demanded I be better, prettier than everyone else in the room. He orchestrated my entire life. He even picked out the man I was to marry."

"Wow. Arranged marriages are still the tradition in other cultures, but in the US? Wow."

"I need you to believe me when I say I didn't know anything about my father trafficking women and selling babies. I didn't."

The bitter, nauseous bile surged up into her throat. Each time she thought about the people her father destroyed, she got queasy.

She hated the pleading in her voice, but she wanted one person—just one person—to believe her.

"I believe you."

A cooling swirl of gratitude soothed the raw, jagged emotional scars. Could he read her mind?

He held out his hand. A lifeline. Her lifeline. She slipped her hand into his warmth.

He didn't say anything. What was there to say?

Seconds ticked by, and time slowed. They gazed at each other, then a slow, friendly smile broke across his face. His honesty and supportive gestures gifted her with a sustaining warmth.

Finally he pointed at the counter. "Our dinner is getting cold."

For a couple of seconds longer she stared at him.

Oh, how she'd like to change—for herself—be the person who could meet a man like Jacob Reyes on the street and be his equal, his partner, his friend.

His gaze dropped, and she realized she was playing with her mother's pendant, the locket that read, "when the storm closes in, believe, for you're brave." The silver locket hovered in the crevice of her breasts. She dropped the chain and pulled her sweater tighter over her chest.

"Ready for dinner?" His eyes rose to hers with a twinkle of a smile.

"Why don't you open the wine?" She handed him the bottle opener. "I've been afraid to drink alone."

"Because you didn't want to get drunk?"

She set the glasses on the table. "Because I don't want to face the ghosts."

He leaned in. "You don't have to be alone if you don't want to."

His breath caressed her skin like a feather, tickling, teasing. *Yes.* She could hear the word in her head, and imagined how easy it would be to give him what he wanted, to take from him what she desired, but she wouldn't slip back into former habits. She'd play it smart. Safe.

"I'm not alone." She nodded toward Dempsey who had curled up on his corner mat to take a nap. "He keeps me busy most of the time. Although he might not be around much longer if he decides to eat another pair of my shoes."

Dempsey chose the moment to stretch and snort.

She rolled her eyes. "Typical guy. He's got me wrapped around his little paw." Just like the computer geek sitting across from her could do so easily. She needed to be careful.

"Family style?" She lifted the takeout bag.

"Sure."

He was wearing the designer jeans from the day they met, but this time he was wearing a button-down shirt, and a pair of three-hundred-dollar calfskin shoes. But he wasn't showing off. He looked comfortable. Perfect. However, his confident expression had slipped a bit, and the vulnerability was downright sexy. He was real, unlike the power-driven, chest-beating men she was determined to avoid.

She unloaded the to-go box and set the food on the table, avoiding the urge to put it in proper serving bowls. He grabbed a spoon and served her first. "Before we were so rudely interrupted, we were discussing your designs."

"Did you like the concept?"

"I told you before, your designs are first-rate." He scooped up a piece of chicken and plopped it on his plate.

The pasta came next. "Have you ever thought about doing some design work for games? You've got a creative mind."

She accepted the plate of cream and buttery richness nestled alongside a selection of spiced tomato savories. "I told you about the crystal city, but I also created another one for my art class. I'd just read Tolkien's books, and decided to create an Elven city. Sort of like Rivendell, only different. This city was built in the clouds."

"Why the clouds?"

"Back then I might have told you it was because I liked the colors of the sunrise and the billowy clouds in the Colorado skies, but if I was honest, I created fantasy worlds as a way to escape. I dreamed up my perfect place—a place where nothing bad ever happened."

Jacob didn't say anything, just waited for her to continue, but she didn't know how much she should say. After all, he was still somewhat of a stranger.

Why had he bought a home in Elkridge?

Where was he going in life?

She should find a way to gracefully step out of his life, let him deal with his friend, and figure out what he wanted to do next, but, as he surmised, there was a pull of attraction she couldn't quite figure out how to ignore.

Heat coursed up her spine.

He provided the same kind of comfort as her favorite pair of slippers warmed by the fireplace heat. He fit—for now— she scolded herself, so why worry about tomorrow?

She cut a bite of chicken, forked it, then added some noodles to her fork.

"If I gave you some specifications"—he talked with his fork waving in the air—"would you be willing to take a stab at drawing a world for me? Something like you talked about. An old idea with a twist?"

"For your video games?"

He nodded.

She shrugged. "Sounds different and fun, as long as you don't mind the designs taking time away from your home redesign."

"I don't mind. Like I told Larson, there's an investor's meeting this coming week, and I desperately need something to present. Does that give you enough time to draw the world?"

She let out a soft laugh. "Yes, although you might care when your home redesign takes longer than you want it to." She turned the fork over and over in her hand, a swell of uneasiness spinning in time. "How will Larson react when he finds out you asked for my help?"

"I'll remind him he didn't deliver. The designs were due last week."

"I don't want to get between the two of you. But if you're positive, I'll start on the designs tomorrow."

The vehemence in his eyes eased. "I usually need a couple of scenery images, then five to seven action sequence frames to get a good idea of a character's movement. However, if we can at least start with some scenery, that should be enough for the investors' meeting. "How does five hundred per story board sound?"

Five? She stared at him. The idea someone would pay her for creating nearly made her jump up and dance around the room. But she wouldn't. The old Rachelle, who had been viciously schooled to hide her emotions, still hadn't conquered her fear of showing how she felt. She tried again to swallow the bite of pasta. "Is five the going rate?"

The corner of his mouth did the little lift and curl she liked. "No. The starting rate is usually three, but I've already seen your work and know what you can do. Plus, I'm desperate. My top designers make a couple grand per sequence, and get a thousand-dollar bonus if their design is selected."

His hand reached out and touched her fingers. "So how about it? Will you help me?"

She turned his hand over, and ran her finger down the center of his palm. His fingers reacted to her touch, but otherwise he waited for her decision. He didn't try to coerce or force her to do the work, and she was grateful, but the skepticism sneaked in anyway.

"Is there a reason you keep throwing money my way?"

He gave a little shrug. "I know what it's like to have your whole world turned upside down."

"Your mom's death."

"Yep." He closed his fingers gently around her hand, massaging her skin with his thumb. "I get the impression you want to do things on your own, yet you need money to get started." He paused to study her. "To be frank, I need the help, and you need the money. Seems like a fair trade to me." His eyes softened, yet didn't hold one grain of sympathy. "So how about it? Will you help?"

Just like that, he melted the shields she forged against the male population she'd sworn to avoid.

"I'll help you, as long as I can trust that when you don't like something, we talk about why the artwork doesn't work."

And, please, no shouting, or hitting, or threatening.

"I keep telling you, I'm not like the other assholes out there who use force to get what they want."

"I didn't say anything about assholes."

His mouth curved. "There's a saying...the eyes are the windows to the soul..."

"Yes, but it is the soul that's the window." She tightened her hand around his. "Or that's what Andrew Hamilton thought, anyway."

He continued rubbing her fingers. "You are the most intriguing woman I've ever met."

"That line's been used before." Disappointment huddled against her ribcage.

"But not from a man who wants nothing more tonight than to sit across the table and have a nice conversation and dinner."

His statement was so genuine she held her breath, daring to hope, dream, there might be a man out there who was real.

She lifted her wine glass. "Then here's to good food, good wine, and good friends."

She could have sworn he hesitated, yet his glass was held up next to hers.

On impulse, she added, "To creativity."

He didn't say a word, only sipped, set down his wine glass, and picked up his fork.

But she wasn't fooled.

Jacob Reyes was the type of man who got what he wanted, even if it took time. And she wasn't sure she disapproved.

When he looked at her, he saw her...her dreams, her fears. He saw right through to her soul.

She'd have to be careful.

Jacob was the kind of man she dreamed about having in her life.

Chapter Eight

"I hear you, Glenn." Jacob paced the length of the mostly empty room. Only a large desk and mesh chair sat at one end of the makeshift office.

"Yes, I will be there Thursday, in person, to present the proposal." His head bobbed like a glass bottle in the ocean. "I know you're getting pressure from the other investors." The muscles in his neck released and his head dropped down. He breathed out a bucketload of frustration. "I'll give you a call tomorrow with an update."

The cell phone beeped a warning. "Glenn, I have another call I need to take. We'll chat soon. 'Bye."

Jacob swiped a thumb across the glass screen to switch calls. "Ben? What's up?"

"Why haven't you returned my call?"

Jacob slumped into his desk chair and rubbed his forehead. He woke up with a headache, and the pain had only intensified.

"Sorry. I've been a little distracted. How are things going with the charity event?"

"Good, if you don't count the fact that the hotel hasn't figured out how to hook up the large screens. I had to call in an electrician. Plus, the hotel caterer had a family emergency and the replacement doesn't know what they're doing. And Dad called. He said he'll be late getting in."

Of course, he'll be late...if he shows up at all.

"Anything else?" Jacob could envision the eye-roll accompanying Ben's humorless laugh.

"Isn't that enough?"

"More than enough." He released a depleting breath. "The investors have scheduled a meeting on Thursday, and they want me to present a draft of what I'm planning."

"That's in just two days. Do you have anything prepared?"

"Not yet. Rachelle has given me some good ideas, though, and has agreed to help." *Or I'd be SOL.* "I left a message for the pilot to see if the plane is available. If not, I'll jump on a commercial flight."

"I know you have a lot on your plate." Ben hesitated, and Jacob could have sworn his brother wanted to add a *but* to the end of the sentence, even though he hadn't said the word aloud.

"Ben, just say what you're thinking."

"Larson's back in town, and he isn't happy. He's been ranting about you adding a new game designer. He says you hired Rachelle without consulting him first. He's pissed."

Jacob pressed his fingers into his temples. "I haven't found a new game designer. He saw some of Rachelle's room designs for the house and jumped to conclusions. Besides, he shouldn't be angry. He hasn't come up with anything, and Rachelle has. She gave me some sample designs yesterday, and I have to tell you, bro, they're good. Good enough to show the investors."

"I told you she was good. Too bad she was forced to liquidate her artwork. It was amazing."

"Artwork? What artwork?"

"Before I hired her, I did a Google search. One of the search results was an eBay auction of her art. There was this one of a clown and a dog, with an Alice in Wonderland-type slant. I put it on my watch list, intending to buy it, but forgot about the auction. I was bummed when I realized I missed bidding."

"Does she have any more art listed?"

"I don't know. She's listed under the name Ovis88."

"I'll check the auction site after I make my flight arrangements. And let me know if there's anything else I need to take care of."

"Will do." Ben hung up, most likely getting distracted by the next thing on his list of to-dos. If nothing else, Ben was efficient.

Jacob glanced at his own list, then shoved the pad away. His mind was getting overly cluttered, and he needed to take a few minutes to streamline his thoughts. Create a plan. Breathe.

In the middle of reshuffling his to-dos a sweet voice wafted through the doorway.

Rachelle. A longing to smell her freshness consumed him.

He shoved away from the desk and made his way toward the kitchen to find her there, leaning over a canvas dog carrier.

Cream-colored lace from her untucked shirt peeked out from under her grapefruit-colored knit sweater. Both covered her rear nicely. The well-loved jeans hugged every curve he'd come to dream about. Oh, and those ankle boots. The image of her in those boots and a bustier and armor fighting through an army of trolls came to mind. She was fierce. Sexy. Stunning.

"You better behave," her voice was stern, but with an air of light humor. "No chewing on anything. You eat one more thing, and I'll paint your toenails pink and put a tutu on you." She waggled her finger. "Trust me. I'll do it."

The French bulldog looked at her, snorted, then waddled toward the kitchen.

"Dempsey, don't you dare give me attitude. There's a dog shelter in town."

The dog sniffed a few cabinets, then flopped to his belly and stretched out his paws.

"That's more like it." Rachelle straightened. "Now be quiet, or you'll get us both booted out of here."

A tug of laugher gurgled in Jacob's throat. He hadn't had something to laugh about for a while, and he was grateful to Rachelle for giving him the gift.

"And why would I kick you out?"

Rachelle spun around to face him. "You *are* here. I called on my way over, but you didn't pick up the phone."

"I had a couple of conference calls this morning."

She moved through the room with caution, like someone might jump out and grab her at any second. The wariness appeared the day Larson showed up and hadn't gone away.

"In case you're wondering, Larson is back in California."

Her violet eyes softened. "You two seem to have a Ben and Jerry thing going on, and I don't want to bust in and take a scoop out of your ice cream bucket, so to speak."

"In many ways, Ben Cohen and Jerry Greenfield are a lot like Larson and me. They're hands-on, like we are with the coders. Like Ben, Larson is the creative, and I manage the people side, like Jerry. Plus, we've been business partners since college." *But it might not last much longer since the jerk can't stay sober.*

Jacob shoved his hands into his pockets and leaned closer to inhale her calming perfume. "I learned a long time ago, I'm good at business, setting a vision for others to follow, and getting things done. However, when it comes to pure creativity, the vision the game is based on, I turn the work over to someone else. I can regurgitate ideas with the best of them, but coming up with something fresh has always been my bane. It's sort of like loving music yet never being able to play the guitar or carry a tune." He shrugged. "I can envision the story, do the coding, but Larson's the one who layered in the world's nuances and made the story come alive."

"So when he saw the designs I created for the house, he assumed the designs were for a new game."

"Something like that. Larson and I have been friends

for a long time, but he can be rather brash." He took her hand. "The next time I talk to him, I'll set him straight."

The concern didn't leave her eyes. "Do you still need something delivered by Thursday?"

"I do. Otherwise, I'm afraid I'll lose funding for my next project."

"I've got more boards to show you." Her heels click, click, clicked across the floor until she stooped to pick up her leather portfolio she'd dropped next to Dempsey's carrier. The air fairly crackled with electricity as she lifted sample boards out of the oversized portfolio bag in one fluid motion. "These are pretty rough, but I think they might spur some ideas." She spread the new set of 8 x 10 boards on the counter.

The design was raw, but the artwork was amazing. The city made of shards of crystals jutted up from the ground. Shades of teal and purple and pink framed the intricate city that sparkled in the mist of clouds.

"Where did you get this?"

"The image has been rolling around my head for years. I just painted what was there. If you like it, I have more from what I've nicknamed my 'mythological collection.' I don't have them with me, but I took some pictures." She grabbed her cell, punched and tapped a few times, then handed him her phone.

A creature—half woman and half bird—appeared first. He swiped his finger across the screen. Lizards and cats and dragons came alive on her phone. The creatures were beautiful, yet in some way sad...lonely.

"All these creatures...they're you," he breathed.

She held out her hand for her phone, and he placed the device in her palm, regretting his hasty words. "I'm duly impressed, but the images won't work for the fan base we've built." He tapped the crystal image again. "This one has potential, though. It's futuristic enough, and so does this one." He enlarged the cloud image. "I think I can work with this. I'll need a couple of characters to fit into these images. Warriors, a couple villains, and of course a hero."

"You mean like this?" She flipped her phone around. The image of a warrior racing through a battlefield with arrows on his back, swords in his hand, his face cloaked by a hood appeared.

Holy shit. "Yes!!! That's perfect, only it needs to be re-designed to fit into a more futuristic world." The hair on his arms raised in salute.

"That shouldn't be a problem." She looked at the phone. "I painted this for my brother's birthday and made him promise never to tell my dad where he got it."

He checked the signature line. "Ovis?"

Rachelle chuckled. "Rachelle means female sheep in Hebrew, and I discovered Ovis means sheep in Latin. My father wanted to be surrounded by all things beautiful, but named me after a farm animal. Ovis was a poke at my dad."

"But why did you make your brother promise never to tell him?"

"Let's just say my father wouldn't have understood my need to create. Interior design is the closest he'd allow me to get to being an artist."

"You could make some big bucks. People eat up this type of artwork."

Excitement flared in her eyes, then died, replaced by wariness. "I'd better stick with the paying jobs for now."

A beam of excitement flashed up his core. "Speaking of jobs. Are you interested in helping me with my presentation?"

"I thought I was. That's why I showed you these boards. They aren't what you need? I should warn you, I can't do graphics."

Yes, you can. "Look, I'm up against a deadline. On Thursday I have to present an idea. *Our* idea. I can't do this without you."

"Thursday?" she choked out. "I thought you just

wanted some ideas. Something you could have your team work on."

"They haven't come up with anything, and your art is just as good as theirs. I was hoping we could work here. I can work on the stories while you draft some backdrops."

She took a couple of steps back and crossed her arms. "Do you know what you're asking? I don't have the proper supplies. I need more canvas boards and paints. Who will turn my artwork into graphics? I certainly don't know how to use graphics programs."

"I've got a team who can translate your artwork. And I'll have whatever you need delivered overnight." He paced back and forth. "You can have my desk. Or take the kitchen table. Your choice. Let's not worry about the graphics. Just focus on the artwork. Make a list of what you need, and I'll get Ben to order the supplies. While you design, I can work on the story." His hands shook with excitement.

For the first time in months, creating a new design didn't seem impossible. His fingers itched to get to a keyboard. Seeing her images had spawned ideas. Battle scenes with winged and four-legged characters tumbled through his mind.

"Whoa. Slow down." She held out her arms in front of her like a traffic cop—only she was trying to stop him.

"We don't have time to slow down. This will work. Trust me." He grabbed Rachelle's hand, pulled, then indulged in a kiss.

Her small initial squeal of surprise instantly turned into a sultry groan. When she fully surrendered, he plunged deeper into her softness. She folded into his arms so perfectly.

When he leaned back, her eyes were closed. Her beauty reminded him of her paintings, colorful and bold, like a rainforest just after a storm.

She tightened her grip on his sleeve.

He angled his head again, this time keeping his kiss

light, and flicked a tongue against her bottom lip, a promise of what could come next. He wanted her—against the wall, breathless, his hands and mouth and body enticing her to respond, winding up their shared sexual tension until they exploded together.

But he waited. Waited for her to decide.

She accepted, absorbed what he gave, but never took the lead the way he expected and encouraged her to do.

The bold, vibrant woman had disappeared.

He lingered a second longer before backing away.

Her eyes flickered open. Her lips were still parted. The pendant on her chest lifted and fell rapidly with each breath.

"Rachelle?" he called to her gently.

She opened her eyes, soft, violet eyes rimmed with dark blue the color of the twilight sky. "Why did you do that? We had an agreement."

There was no resentment, or anger, only wonderment.

"You're right. I shouldn't have kissed you. And I would apologize if I didn't think you also feel something." He'd wanted to kiss her since the first day he set eyes on her. "Rachelle, tell me you're not interested, and I will never touch you again. Promise."

Her brows drew together, then loosened in an emotional tug of war. "I can't."

He couldn't stop the smile from making his mouth do a little curl. "Then would you mind if I kiss you again?"

She arched back. "Maybe later." She released her fingers, as if realizing she had a death-grip on his arm. "Right now we have work to do."

"The work can wait."

"No it can't. Thursday is just two days away." She closed her eyes, yet her facial muscles conveyed she was still thinking. Eventually her eyes popped open. "Okay. You get started on the story while I go home to pack up my supplies and get us some lunch."

He leaned in and kissed her nose. "Deal."

"Do you mind if I leave Dempsey here?"

The dog now lay curled up on the living room couch, and didn't budge.

"Leave him. He looks comfortable."

She stepped around him, making a wide arc to grab her purse and keys, and headed for the door.

He tried to ignore the deflating sizzle in his groin, because she was right. He had work to do, but that didn't mean he didn't want to indulge in Rachelle Clairemont's creativity.

He liked the way she looked at him. Not the millionaire. Not the computer geek—just a man who wanted to build something amazing with her.

At least he hoped it would be amazing.

Chapter Nine

Rachelle grabbed the lunch and painting supplies from her back seat. The bags felt like bricks in her hands.

What was she thinking?

Designing the futuristic graphics was just another project she put her heart and soul into, and then someone else would take the credit.

For years she made her father look good. She planned dinner parties, exquisite outings, and charity events and never received credit for a single one of them.

Uuuggghhh. She wanted to scream.

She had to stop thinking about that man.

Her father had woven around every organ in her body like a parasite. He slowed her down, made her question every action. She wanted a cure—now—because her gut told her this project was different.

She would get to explore art out in the open.

Show off her artwork.

Jacob appreciated her craft. He even said as much.

The look on his face when she showed him the sample boards was priceless. Even though he didn't think the forest creatures would work, he liked those as well. She had painted what was in her soul. A beautiful bird trapped in a cage. A brave feline collared with chains. He saw through the imagery immediately and understood.

He only had two days.

For two days she could indulge, immerse herself in an imaginary world, revel in the luxury of being able to create and explore. Painting for hours and hours without listening for an odd sound, or a door to open, or feeling anxious.

Dempsey met her at the door, sniffed her foot, then trotted toward the kitchen.

"You're back," Jacob took the heavier supply bag from her arms.

The kitchen table had been cleared of place mats. His laptop was open on one side. She assumed she'd be sitting on the other. The open kitchen window shades let in the afternoon sun, casting the perfect amount of light.

She raised the bag filled with deli salads, sandwiches, and a couple of cans of dog food for Dempsey. "Lunch?"

"Do you mind if we eat while we work? I'd like to get started." She swore he almost skipped to the kitchen table.

"Do you have something I can use for Dempsey's lunch?"

He opened the cabinet and lifted a side plate off the top of the stack.

Her insides squinched. She should use the salad container, or the lunch wrap, or go back to her house to get the dog bowl, not a proper plate. Then, banishing her old ways to the time-out corner, she reached for the offered plate. "Dempsey? Lunch."

Small claws clicked eagerly along the floor, and the bulldog sat next to her, waiting for his grub. When she lifted the plate, he whirled around in a circle with a can't-wait-can't-wait whine.

"Here you go." She brushed a hand down his soft, furry back. "You're a good boy."

He ignored her and lapped up the beef in gravy.

"What can I help with?" She rinsed the spoon in the sink with soap before dropping it in the silverware holder in the dishwasher.

"I got this," Jacob placed half of each sandwich on a plate. "Get yourself whatever you want to drink. I put some bottles of tea and flavored water in the beverage fridge."

When she took a seat at the glass table with a modern chrome base, he set a plate, along with a napkin, by her elbow.

"First things first. I talked to Ben. Just give him a list of what you need. He confirmed he'll have your supplies delivered first thing in the morning."

"You sure? Overnight shipping will be expensive."

"If I don't nail this investor meeting...*that* will be expensive."

She retrieved her notebook and ripped out a sheet.

"What's all that?" He pointed to a page filled with swirls and loops and symbols.

"This?" She pointed at the page. "It's like shorthand, only different."

"How different?"

"Each of these symbols means something different, and only I can read what's on the page. It's like a secret code."

"What's it say?"

She placed her finger on the top left symbol. "It says Jacob Reyes. Mother died when fourteen. Moved from Calgary to California. Lived with dad and stepmom in Silicon Valley. Dad worked for major electronics company in the R&D department. Jacob attended University of Southern California. He wears a lot of grey. Likes mythical creatures and dragons. Vanilla bean coffee creamer. Clean lines. Wears watches—expensive watches—Rolex, Movado, Fossil, Franck Muller." She pressed a finger to the place she stopped. "Do you want me to go on?"

"That's sort of spooky."

"Have you ever Googled yourself? You have a full Wikipedia page, and your Facebook profile isn't locked down. Plus you love to chat about food on Twitter. If you don't want people poking into your life, lock down your social media pages."

"No, I meant it's awesome. You have this whole language you can read. It's like Dothraki, or Klingon, or Elvish."

"Yes, but those languages are both written and verbal. This is only written."

"Can anyone read what you write?"

She shook her head. "Not without a key."

"Where's the key?"

She tapped her fingers on the page. Should she tell him? It wouldn't hurt. Besides, no one had ever been able to find her journals, not even the FBI. "The key is in my head. A long time ago, I realized, after my brother stole my diary, that the only way to keep anything written secret was to memorize the key."

"That's so cool." He dropped his plate on the other side of the table. "We better get working. First things first. Send your supply list to Ben—in English," he winked. "I want to make sure he can get what you need."

She jotted down a few items, then added a few more.

As the day progressed, the table filled with coffee cups and discarded paper towels with test paint splotches and bags of chips. Whatever she needed appeared.

Her heart soared with unlimited bliss. She painted until her hands cramped and her back ached, yet she couldn't stop. Periodically, she'd pause to listen to Jacob's story and make suggestions, then would go right back to work.

When the lighting no longer worked, lamps were relocated. And the work continued.

"How's it going?" Jacob reached toward the ceiling and stretched, letting his head fall to one side then the other.

"I almost have the second set done." She dabbed her brush in water, then brushed it back and forth on the towel to rid the brush of the acrylic pigment. "These really should be done in oil, but we don't have time for the paint to dry."

"They look great, and the investors will get the gist." He stood to stretch his back. "Hungry?"

"Lord, no. I've eaten more junk food today than in the whole rest of my life." She picked up a rag to clean a paint splash off the glass table. "What time is it?"

"A little past eleven."

"Eleven?" She stared past the lamps toward the picture windows at the night sky. The moon had already risen past the highest pane. All she saw were the stars. "I should go."

"Why? There are clean sheets on Ben's bed. You can stay in his room."

She did hate to drive at night. Plus, the drive to her cabin wasn't lit, and there were always skunks and other animals about. But still.

"I'll be okay."

"You might, but Dempsey might not. He looks rather comfortable."

Her pup was upside down, with all four paws in the air, fast asleep. He looked so cute with his pink jowls hanging down and his tongue sticking out.

"I don't want to cause you any trouble."

"Seriously? You're the one doing me a favor, here. The least I can do is offer you somewhere to sleep after working all day and half the night. Come on, stay. I'll find some sweats and a T-shirt. I even have some of those travel-sized shampoos and conditioners. You can take your pick."

"If you're sure it won't be any trouble."

He moved closer and ran the backs of his knuckles down her cheek. She must have been tired, because she leaned in and let him hold the weight of her head. She closed her eyes, and took in his warmth, letting her breathing slow.

"Let's get you to bed."

Her eyes popped open when he reached for her hand, and she automatically recoiled. "I...um...I'm good."

"No you're not. You practically fell asleep sitting up. I'm not letting you drive home." He took a step back. "Ben's room is at the top of the stairs on the left."

My old room. When she stood, he didn't move. He smelled like corn chips and beer. The combination made her want to lick his lips. She preferred salty over sweet, and she imagined Jacob was a perfect salt lick.

Oh, God. I must be tired.

"What time do you want to start in the morning?"

"No particular time. Whenever you get up."

He lifted her hand to his lips. "Goodnight, Rachelle, and thank you. Your work is amazing, and so are you." His thumb caressed her cheek, and his voice had deepened with yearning.

The praise made her shields of power dim. She should keep them in place, but somehow this gamer had found a way to bypass her circuit controls.

"Jacob, you promised."

His thumb paused, then pressed lightly into her chin. "Yes, I did make you a promise. And as hard as the promise will be to keep, I will, just to prove I'm different."

He might keep the promise, but she wasn't certain she wanted him to.

"Good night, Jacob."

"Good night, Goldilocks," he smiled, and her mind tripped over the nickname, but she walked past him and kept on walking. If she had turned around, her heart would have made her walk right back into his arms.

Chapter Ten

Rachelle awoke to a sky illuminated with sunrise pinks and burning, bright oranges and purples. The colors crisscrossed the bank of bedroom windows, which looked out over the mountain ridge. She loved lying in this bed, watching the finches fly from one spruce tree to another.

She waited for the squirrel to hop along the deck railing toward his feeder, then remembered it was no longer there.

This wasn't her home. This wasn't her room. This wasn't her life.

She tossed back the bedding and climbed out of bed, grabbing her hairband to bundle her hair up on top of her head.

She needed to get Jacob on his way so she could get back to looking for long-term work. If she only did one room at a time, then maybe when she found work, she could turn the project over to someone else.

That's what she would do.

First, she needed to get two more storyboard sequences done, and then she'd be free again.

She shoved her feet into a pair of wool socks and made her way to the kitchen to find Dempsey.

She was halfway down the stairs, when he found her.

"There you are. Want some breakfast?"

With a snort and a turn, he trotted off to wait by his newly acquired dinner plate.

She opened the pantry door, then paused while her mind reset.

"Right. Not my home." She backed out and shut the door before turning to the island and the stack of cans. *I've got to get out of here.*

Her gut tightened, but she set the unsettled feeling aside and spooned the brown, wet clumps on the plate. "This stuff smells disgusting. Sit."

Dempsey waited while she lowered the plate. "Good boy." She patted him on the head, but he ignored her again and dug into his grub. If only she could be so singularly focused.

She lifted the can to read the label and occupy her mind. "Combines two popular flavors that will leave the dog's tail wagging all day."

"Right. My dog doesn't have a tail."

She reached in the drawer for some tinfoil and came up with sandwich bags. "I guess this will do."

She shoved the plastic over the top of the can, sealed it, and stashed it in the refrigerator.

"I definitely need to get out of here." She slid the kitchen chair back, grabbed a sketching pencil, and got to work, ignoring her caffeine-depleted headache.

Minutes ticked by while she drew and discarded, then started again, until an idea clicked.

"That's perfect."

Her hand jerked, but she picked up the pencil just in time to save the outline of a character who looked like a cross between Lara Croft and the Norse goddess Frigga, Odin's wife...or her versions anyway.

"I didn't hear you come down."

"You must not have heard me talking to Dempsey either, then."

"I didn't." She picked up her eraser. "Anything you want changed?"

"Nope. I love your work." He pointed at the warrior's armor. "I love the Celtic design here."

"It's actually Norse influence," she corrected, then automatically flinched, wondering if there would be a backlash, then chastised herself for reacting.

Jacob wouldn't hurt her. He created a cozy, comfortable ambiance. She loved how he respected her space, yet remained snugly on the fringe, within easy reach. But she didn't want to indulge in his hospitality.

He set a cup of coffee by her elbow, and the soothing aroma of almonds wafted around her. Correct that. Not all aspects of his hospitality.

He reached across the table to tap his computer to boot, then scratched his chin, his eyes barely open. "I can't wait for you to show your stuff to the design team."

"Me?" Her voice scaled up an octave. "Isn't your team in California?"

"They are. I thought we could fly out for the meeting tomorrow, and then you could stick around, meet the team and attend the charity lunch."

He couldn't be serious. She turned in her chair to look up at him. He was serious. "You want me to go with you...to California."

"It will be fun."

Fun? Getting on an airplane with some guy she just met, to go to a business meeting with people she didn't know, then meet with the creative team...who might or might not like her work. That didn't sound like fun. It sounded scary.

"What's wrong?" He tucked a strand of hair that had fallen in her face behind her ear.

Could she tell him? No...it was way too revealing. "I...uh...I need to work on your room designs. Your house is half furnished. You can't live in this chaotic mess." She grabbed hold of the excuse like it was a lifeline.

"You don't want to come with me?"

"You'll do fine." She held her breath, hoping her act was convincing.

He leaned and picked up her hand, rubbing a thumb over her wrist. "I'd like you to be there. The reason I'm able to do the presentation at all is because you were willing to work on the designs. The rest of the team came up empty, or regurgitated what we've already done.

"I don't want to be sued for copyright infringement after selling my game. Your images help me see a different story. Plus, you're the one who came up with the challenge level details. I've just incorporated the details into the storyboards."

Rachelle tried again to stomp out the fear growing inside. Jacob had given her no reason to fear he was anything other than an even-tempered man. Then again, anything could happen to spin calm out of control. Being at someone else's mercy terrified her.

"I can see you're uncomfortable." He dropped her hand to retrieve his phone. "I don't want to present without you there. I'll cancel the meeting."

He scrolled to dial, but she reached out a hand. "Wait."

He studied her face, but remained silent.

"I'll go." The acceptance tumbled out all smashed together, as if she'd change her mind if she had any time to think.

"Are you sure? I wouldn't want to put you into an uncomfortable position."

She shoved her pencil into her bun. He could see her vulnerabilities, and she hated being exposed that way. She would never have shown weakness in her father's presence, but Jacob was different. He disarmed her. Allowed her to get comfortable. Somehow permitted her to be flawed.

"I'm okay."

He raised her hand to his warm lips, placing them on her wrist. When his tongue caressed her skin, a tingling sensation spiraled up from her fingers and toes.

"You're more than just okay, Rachelle."

She laughed off his praise. "I bet you say that to all the women."

"I told you before, I haven't had many women in my

life."

"Their loss. Someday you'll find a cover model, or an entrepreneur intent on saving the world, or some other interesting, sophisticated woman who deserves you."

He rolled his eyes. "I don't have time to play games. I need to spend my time making them." He laughed at his own pun.

She stared at him. Was he serious? "Why? With your looks and personality," *and money*, which carefully she didn't add to the list, "you could take your pick. You're a great guy. You should find someone. Be happy."

"Now you're starting to sound like Ben." He strolled over to the floor-to-ceiling window and stood quietly with his hands shoved in his pockets. "I was in love once."

A crack in his voice tempted her curiosity. "What happened?"

He shrugged and shoved his hands deeper into his pockets. "She decided a football jock was a lot more fun than an IT geek."

"She dumped you?"

His eyes flashed. "Ouch-crash-boom-whollup." He attempted a comic book smile.

She turned in her chair, debating whether or not to reach out. "Some women are just plain stupid."

"You think?" He fought off a smile.

"Yes, I know. They think hot bad boys are the way to go, until they get handled a bit too roughly. Men like to own, dominate, crush."

"Not all men. I keep telling you, I'm not one of those guys."

He also wasn't a hookup type who subscribed to every dating app and right-swiped on every picture to increase his odds of getting lucky.

"I can still cancel if you're uncomfortable." His intense, green-speckled hazel gaze sliced through her concerns. "But I'd rather not. Rachelle, please come with me to California to help me present and meet the team."

No. Just say no. "It's only for a few days, right?"

He walked toward her slowly. "Just a couple."

"Okay."

He leaned in. "I so want to kiss you now."

"Your kisses are becoming a habit."

He leaned a little closer. "Habits aren't always bad for you, you know."

Either his words or his hot, coffee-fragrant breath were the cause of the tingles shimmering down her neck, and the reason she closed the two-inch gap. He responded with the richest, sexiest kiss she'd ever experienced.

She kissed him back, this man of her choosing—not of her father's, or anyone else's.

Her mind echoed with the word *yes*.

Chapter Eleven

Rachelle clutched the armrest of her airplane seat as the small executive plane descended.

Why did she ever agree to get on the plane? Her whole world was again spinning out of control. Houses, a baseball field, and the ocean crowded the view. She couldn't see the runway yet, but expected it was just ahead.

"Remind me to call and check on Dempsey after we land."

Jacob sat across from her, oblivious to the descent, too busy doing last-minute adjustments to his presentation.

"He'll be fine at the kennel. He's got plenty of dogs to play with. Didn't you say you know the owner?"

"Karly Krane. We went to school together."

"See? He'll be fine."

No, he won't. He doesn't play well with others. He's like me. In a way, Dempsey was a lot like her brother as well. He acted out to get attention because he wanted more attention than any one person could give.

She pressed back into the oversized leather seat and studied Jacob. He sat across from her with a small table in between them, focusing on his laptop. Their drinks had been cleared by a crewmember twenty minutes earlier, but now she wished she'd asked for ginger ale to settle her stomach.

"Are you comfortable with the presentation?" she asked, digging her fingers into the armrest when the small jet hit the runway and bounced.

"Yep, just trying to make sure I've covered potential

questions the investment team may ask. One can never be too prepared."

How can you be so calm?

"Mr. Reyes," Captain Norris's baritone announced through the speaker, "I've confirmed your limousine is waiting. Give us a few minutes to park and let the crew unlock the doors for your departure. The weather is sixty-three degrees with a slight wind out of the west. The driver would like you to know there is no traffic. You should reach your meeting on time." Jacob pressed the intercom button on the side of his chair. "Thanks, Doug. Nice flight."

Nice flight? What was he talking about?

Her stomach felt like she'd been bouncing on a trampoline for the past two hours.

"You'll do great." She wanted to reach out and touch his arm, needing to tap into his tranquility, but pressed back into her seat.

"*We* will do great. I'm not worried. The concept is solid. If they don't want to back me, someone else will." His vibrato sounded solid, but he was concerned about the capital, she could tell by the way he was studying the presentation to make sure every nuance was addressed.

She folded up the lap blanket and laid the plush throw on the seat across the aisle to give herself something else to think about.

"You sound confident." She'd straightened the jacket of her royal blue suit with silver accents. The power suit would make a statement. One Jacob had already noticed. He'd changed mid-flight into a blue suit and open-collared button-down. He looked like the effective CEO his title declared him to be.

"That's my job. I have to champion my business. No one else will."

He waited for her to join him at the front of the cabin, then let her exit the plane first. A chauffeur held the limo door open, and she slid into the black leather interior.

"Ben." Her breath caught in her chest, then was quickly followed with a joyous exhale. "I wasn't expecting to see you."

"Holding my brother hostage is the only way I can pin him down long enough to get answers. This is probably the last chance I'll get before the charity event on Saturday."

As soon as Jacob slid into the seat and the car door shut, Ben launched into his update. Jacob's eyes had glazed over after thirty seconds.

"Lastly, we might need to hire extra help," Ben leaned forward and tapped his brother on the knee. "Did you hear what I said?"

Rachelle pulled a pad of paper from her purse. "Since the hotel doesn't have enough kids' chairs, may I suggest someone purchase yoga balls. They come in all different colors and sizes. I suggest getting a small size and an air pump. The kids will love sitting on them. Plus, you can even give them away if you want, as prizes or something." She took a breath and jotted down some notes. "It's unfortunate the hotel's kitchen caught fire. I say we contact a fast food restaurant and bring in chicken nuggets or something similar. We can get ice from the hotel, and bring in sodas and ice cream and different kinds of chips." She added a few more items to the list, then looked up.

Both men were staring at her wide-eyed. "I...uhhh...never mind." She slid the pad back into her purse and folded her hands in her lap.

Ben turned to Jacob. "If you don't kiss this woman, I will, and I don't kiss women very often."

She threw him a grateful glance. "I tend to take over. You don't mind?"

"Woman, you're a miracle worker. I love you." Ben grabbed her hand and kissed each one of her fingers. When he began the second round, making exaggerated smooching sounds, she tried pulling her hand back.

"Stop!" The wimpy demand fizzled with another giggle.

Only Jacob's low, resonating, possessive growl made Ben release her hand.

Jacob leaned closer to her ear. "I'll thank you properly when we get home tonight, and I won't be kissing just your fingers." He slid her a sly warning, which made her core overheat.

"This is a business trip," she reminded him.

"Yes, and after that part is over," he lowered his voice to a whisper, "I would like to celebrate. One way or another, the two of us together is a winning combination," he breathed in her ear, each word sending a shiver down her spine.

Ohhh. Stay calm. Breathe. She crossed her legs to stifle the throb of heat from what he whispered.

Ben tapped her knee to get her attention. "Ms. Problem-Solver, I have another problem for you to solve."

Thankful for the reprieve, she engaged Ben in back-and-forth banter for another ten minutes, until the limo pulled up in front of an impressive business complex.

"Did we cover everything?" Rachelle ripped off the to-do list and handed it to Ben. She liked Jacob's brother, and loved being able to help the kids.

"You might regret giving me your cell phone number."

"I'm here if you need me." Rachelle chuckled, and accepted Jacob's hand to exit the car.

Ben leaned out of the car. "Marry this one, would you?"

Panic seized her breath.

Ben pulled the door shut, and a second later the limousine merged into traffic.

Jacob, preoccupied with his presentation preparations, absentmindedly interlaced his fingers into hers and tugged. "Come on, we need to get going if we don't want to be late."

She numbly followed him through the rotating doors to the elevators, all the while struggling to rid her mind of the thought of marriage.

Instead, she visualized the presentation sequence, letting each slide and graphic materialize, but the images kept shifting out of focus. His warm skin against hers messed with her concentration. She could smell his scent, which reminded her of an ocean breeze. His presence soothed her, made her believe in goodness and possibilities.

When the elevator doors opened, he entered, pulling her along, then pushed the button to the top floor. "You'll like Glenn." Jacob adjusted his suit jacket in the mirrored elevator walls. "The other investors are financial types who like to flash their money around."

The undertone of his statement caused her internal system to blare a warning. The elevator door opened, and he walked to the towering glass doors with the names of several organizations she didn't recognize.

A receptionist stood and escorted them into a vast boardroom overlooking the city of San Diego. Another visitor might have been impressed, but she wasn't. The black leather high-back chairs and neutral color carpeting set a boring mood. There was no energy—no spark—no personality. The design left the room nondescript, blah. The room, clearly meant to impress, was just another expensive but plain room just like all the other boardrooms she'd visited.

Yet instinct told her Jacob would create the fireworks. He didn't hesitate, just pulled his laptop out of his bag and connected it to the room's projection system. His company logo flashed across the video screen.

"Jacob. You're here." A tall man in his late fifties entered the room from the far end. "I wasn't sure you would make it."

"I told you I'd be here." Jacob placed a hand on the small of Rachelle's back, a possessive gesture, but she didn't mind, especially since the three men following Glenn into the conference room fit the profile of men she desperately tried to avoid. Dark suits, greedy eyes, pompous smirks. The way their eyes skimmed over her made her feel dirty.

She tapped into the warmth emanating from Jacob's touch, fighting against the urge to leave.

Jacob stepped in front of her, shaking hands, and directed the men to the other side of the table, away from her. "Gentlemen, shall we get started?"

Her breath had gone shallow until she caught the look in Jacob's eye, a look that said, *I'm here, you're safe.*

The word *safe* echoed in her mind and bounced her out of a fear-induced trance which had lasted only a microsecond. She forged a smile and handed Jacob the stack of portfolios of company information, financials, and the slide deck she'd collated.

Jacob gestured for her to occupy the chair next to him and took a position at the front of the room. His shoulders back. His chin confident.

He began his presentation with a joke to lighten the mood. His vocal cadence was brilliant, engaging. She admired how he created his story and pulled the investors into the imagery of his world. He used her art to visually support his narrative. And then his presentation crescendoed into a dazzling summation.

She released a heavy sigh, unaware her previous shallow breaths hadn't provided enough oxygen.

The men around the table shifted with non-verbal approval on their faces.

"Bravo," Glenn said. "Very nice."

Jacob let his gaze fall to her mouth, his expression telling her how much he wanted to kiss her.

He turned when he heard an investor ask a question. "I'm sorry. What was your question?"

"Where did you come up with these scenes?" The older man at the end of the table reminded her of Grumpy Cat. His forehead and mouth seemed set in a permanent scowl, and his eyes were expressly disinterested.

He turned up his nose. "I haven't seen anything like this on the market."

Surprise swizzled up her arms.

Jacob again met her gaze, his features soft, supportive. "I'd like Rachelle to answer your question. She designed the picture you're holding, and is the best person to respond."

A ribbon of amazement twirled through her chest. He'd given her credit.

No one had ever given her credit. Ever—for anything.

In her former world, a woman's duty was to remain silently behind the scenes.

Always supportive.

A beautiful face to be seen. But never heard.

She'd worked years to make business meetings and social engagements seem effortless. Flawless.

Rachelle got to her feet, and Jacob backed up the presentation to the first artwork slide. She lifted her chin and proceeded to provide the roots of her design ideas, proving the concepts were singularly hers.

"Please tell me you have this woman under an exclusive contract, Jacob."

Jacob broke into a grin. "Not yet, but I'm working on it."

"Glenn?" The older investor closed his portfolio and stood, his permanent scowl still in place. "We have a lunch meeting." Mr. Crankypants strolled to the doorway, talking to his colleagues, then stood to the side to let the others leave before turning back. "Jacob, we'll give you a call once we've made a decision."

"Thank you for your time."

Glenn extended his hand toward Rachelle. "Nice job, young lady." He winked. "If Jacob isn't your type, I've got a son I would like to introduce you to. How about dinner tomorrow night?"

Jacob stepped in. "We have plans."

"How about Saturday then?"

"Saturday is the charity event I'm hosting. I'm expecting to see you and your wife there, since you're one of the main sponsors."

"Right."

Glenn's tanned skin made the corners of his eyes crinkle. His silver-green eyes danced with a bit of humor when he delivered another wink, knowing he was pushing his young mentoree's buttons. "I'm serious, young lady. If this one doesn't treat you right, you call me. I'll set him straight."

She laughed at his California charm.

Jacob sliced the older gentleman with a look. "I thought you were on my side."

"Admit it." Glenn intervened. "You're a workaholic, and this pretty lady is too beautiful to be ignored."

Jacob packed his computer in his bag. "You can say whatever you like about me, but Rachelle makes up her own mind. She picked me, and I'm pleased she did."

Did I? When?

Glenn held out his hand. "Can't blame a Dad for trying." Glenn stepped to the door of the boardroom. "Rachelle, it's nice meeting you. I have a feeling over time I'll get to see a lot of you."

What did Glenn mean? She wasn't moving to San Diego. No way could she afford to live in California.

Glenn disappeared before she could ask him to clarify. Jacob took a step closer. "We did it."

"You did it."

"Oh, no." He let out a little snort of surprise. "This was a team effort, and you were brilliant."

Her eyebrows shot up. "Me?"

"You. Where have you been all my life?"

Hidden away. Just the way my father wanted. Her composure slipped a bit, and she nervously smoothed her dress. She defaulted to her plastic mute smile.

He leaned in. "Hungry?"

Yes, for another of your sweet kisses. Heat flared up

her cheeks at the thought. Jacob fought back a smile, as if he knew what she'd been thinking.

"Do you like fish tacos?"

Her mind got stuck on the words tacos and fish combined in a single sentence. "I don't think I've ever had fish tacos."

"No?" He walked her to the elevator. "Then you will love this restaurant. It's a tiny place, maybe ten tables, and they serve the best tacos, with this tangy cabbage. Guaranteed, it will be unforgettable."

If the cabbage is anything like your tangy kisses, I think you'd be right.

He settled in close enough for her to take in his spicy scent, a smell she could wake up to every morning.

What? Wait a minute.

Her mind frantically tried to backspace and delete the thought, but the desire was already out there and permanent.

She felt his hand settle on her lower back, but continued walking. Once they were through the rotating doors, Jacob approached the waiting limousine. Something inside her rejected the idea of getting in a hot car on such a glorious day.

"How far is it to the restaurant?" she asked.

"About ten blocks or so."

"Do you mind if we walk?" His eyes held a question. "The sun is shining, I've never been here before, and the architecture seems amazing. Do you mind?"

He looked at her feet and three-inch heels. "Are you sure? Those stilts look a bit uncomfortable."

She reached into her bag and pulled out a pair of sandals. "I'm always prepared."

"Yes, you are." He waved the driver away. "Why not?"

She reached up and fluffed her heavily styled hair, making the curls a bit messy.

Jacob's focus intensified, even though his hand moved lazily up and down her arm.

Could she indulge? Right there on the street. Should she wrap her arms around him, and never let go?

The idea of a public display of affection terrified her.

Would he get the wrong idea?

What if she was wrong about him? What if San Diego, the meeting, the charity event, were all just part of a psychopathic ploy?

She took a step back, "Ready?"

"Definitely." His intimate tone warmed her womanly bits.

Oh, man. She was in deep, deep trouble.

Chapter Twelve

The family strolling along the sidewalk in front of Jacob exposed a void he never realized existed.

The father with a baby strapped to his chest, holding the hand of a mother pushing what looked like a two-year-old, made him want a family—more than ever. The group wasn't in a hurry. Likely there was no place they needed to be other than in each other's company.

He'd never envisioned marriage, and certainly not kids, until recently.

He reached for Rachelle's hand, letting their fingers interlock so naturally.

Plenty of women wanted to connect with him, especially after the sale of his game was splashed across the internet. However, they only wanted to know his bank account balance and have a good time. Sex for the sake of sex wasn't a game he liked to play.

Wasn't it ironic? The one thing that attracted other women repelled Rachelle.

He squeezed her hand, and she looked in his direction. "Is everything all right?"

"Just thinking about life." He chuckled at the irony. "Pretty heavy subject for a beautiful day like today."

She fought to constrain the wisps of hair riding on the current of wind coming from the sea, but she gave up after a few seconds, and let their interlocked hands swing gently back and forth in time with their steps.

"I used to play this game with myself," she pointed to an elderly couple sitting on a bench, sharing a basket of fried clams and chips. "I would pick out some people in a restaurant or at the mall. I'd imagine what my life would have been like if I were a part of their family. Like, would I have gone to college, or learned to play the piano, or would I be married with three kids?"

"Wait a minute," he tugged on her arm, "You didn't go to college?"

"Aren't you the education snob?" A light, teasing tone got hitched onto her statement, but he could see her cloaking mask slip into place.

"What I meant was, you know foreign languages, history, art, and are pretty much one of the smartest people I know. I shouldn't have made an assumption. My bad. I'm just surprised, that's all."

Her mouth opened, then closed. She was thinking about her response. He could tell by the grip of her hand getting tighter and tighter.

"Rachelle?" He stopped at a cross street to wait for the light. "What did I say that upset you?"

"Nothing." The flashed expression told him otherwise. The walk signal turned green, and she took a step off the curb.

"Did I remember to tell you how much I appreciated your help today?" he offered, trying to restart the conversation. "Well, really, for the last several days? You nailed it."

"You nailed it." A subtle shift in her voice ignited a spurt of energy. Her dragging steps picked up the pace, and her arms swung more freely. A question settled into her eyes before she turned away.

"Ask your question, Rachelle."

Her focus shifted again to study his face. He could have sworn disappointment flashed in her eyes. The old feeling of inadequacy popped up like a clown in a jack-in-the-box, but he stuffed the clown's head back in the box as fast as it had appeared.

He didn't have room in his life for insecurities anymore.

He slowed his steps, "Rachelle? What are you thinking?"

"I did a lot of background research on you to create a design you would like. You show the world an image of yourself, but I have a strong impression that no one really knows you."

"Let me see if I can correct your opinion." A seagull squawked and dropped down to pick up scraps of food, then flew off again. He took a few more steps. "I loved living in Canada. The people and the way of life are different, and I would have stayed if not for my dad. He always wanted more. What's not in your fact sheet is my dad just left us one day. He was offered a job in the US, and just left, without talking to my mom. He was there one day, then gone the next."

"Did you ever see him?"

Jacob shrugged. "He'd call and email once in a while. Later on I found out he'd been having an affair with one of his colleagues, and he moved to California to be with her."

"That must have been rough."

"It brought me and my mom closer." He pointed out the USS Midway, but kept strolling along with the crowds of tourists meandering along the waterway. "For years we used to go several days a week for her kidney dialysis treatments. The appointments would last for hours, and I would sit by her side and read or play video games."

He took a deep breath, but the reaction wasn't burdened, just the opposite. She moved in closer, which encouraged him to continue.

"After she was done, I'd drive her home." He chuckled, but humor didn't come along for the ride. "I had to sit up tall to see over the steering wheel."

She turned to him, her eyes narrowed with confusion. "I thought you relocated to the US when you were fourteen."

"I did. After my mom got sick, we found an apartment

close to the hospital. I was always careful not to get caught driving."

She turned her face up toward the sun to soak in the rays. "I can't imagine emigrating to a different country. Plus, you didn't know your dad, and it seems he had a new family."

"Ben was only seven when I arrived." Jacob smiled at the memory of their first meeting. His new brother looked pleased to have an ally in the house. "He was like my little shadow, following me everywhere."

"My dad was pretty hard on my brother," Rachelle's voice dropped to almost a whisper. "Brad grew up angry. As a result, he did a lot of things he wasn't proud of."

Jacob slowed his steps to a crawl. "Where was your mom?"

"She left. My dad can be pretty demanding. That's why I was never allowed to go to college. He never wanted to be alone."

Rachelle tried pulling away, but he held on. There were questions he wanted to ask, but now wasn't the time or place. He wanted to be there for her, no matter what, and he wouldn't judge. She didn't need to be alone, trapped in her past.

The warmth from her fingers pressed against his skin, sending a laser beam of happiness up his arms and exploding into his chest. He couldn't hold back his feelings. He was damn sure his heart had just taken the deep dive into the love pool.

He wanted to protect, not control. "From what I understand, your dad's no longer in the picture."

She studied him for a long moment, then they were interrupted by a couple of bicycle-taxis passing by. "I don't think I'll ever see my father again. He's serving several life sentences without the possibility of parole." Her face paled. "Maybe being associated with me isn't a good idea. If someone finds out who I am, or the press gets a hold of the story—"

"Then I'll deal with it. Larson and I have a marketing team who manages those sorts of things."

He could see her wanting to ask questions about his buddy, but she didn't, and he was grateful, because he wasn't sure just yet what he was going to do about Larson's relapse.

The wind picked up again, and she tried but failed to tuck her hair back, then he spotted the small sheen of a tear. He pulled her to him.

"Rachelle, I'm sorry if—" She tried to push out of his arms, but her attempt stalled when he gently tightened his arms. "It's okay." He laid his cheek on top of her head, wrapping his body around hers.

"I don't know why I'm crying." She arched back to press her fingertips under her eyes. "I never cry, but I've been crying a lot lately."

He tucked her hair behind her ears and lifted her face to look into her eyes. "Is it because you've never been allowed to cry?"

"See? That's why I'm crying." Her emotions warped her face into utter sorrow. "Today is the first time in my life I've been allowed to be who I am on the inside. I've exposed myself, and no one has scolded or punished me. I felt safe. No"—she shook her head—"It's more than that." Her eyes met his. "I feel alive. You make me feel alive."

He lifted his hands to hold her hair so he could see into her beautiful eyes. "No, Rachelle. It's not because of me. It's because of you. You're one helluva brave woman."

"I'm not brave. Just careful. I learned to adapt. Hide. Be what my father expected."

"And in turn you lost who you were."

Everything within her heart rejected the idea. "You can't lose what you never found in the first place."

Jacob leaned in and captured her sweet lips, then lifted and brushed her nose with the tip of his. "Then today we certainly have a reason to celebrate. Today is the first day you get to be the true Rachelle Clairemont."

Fear welled in her eyes.

He settled an arm around her shoulder and continued at a slow pace along the promenade. "Picture this." He used his hand to brush a rainbow arc in front of them. "Fish Tacos. The San Diego Zoo." He turned around and started walking backward and pulling her along. "Hanging out in the Gaslight district." His eyes opened wider. "A romantic harbor cruise at sunset." Finally, there was the laugh he wanted. "If nothing sounds appealing, how about a baseball game?"

"What, no video games?"

He stopped, and she bumped into him. He was quick to wrap his arms around her waist. "Woman, you're going to make me a better man. I just know it."

"I doubt that, but I am sure you're going to kiss me right now."

He didn't hesitate. He wove his fingers into her hair, and indulged for just a second, before pulling back. "Tacos."

"What?" Confusion glazed over her eyes.

"I'm hungry for guacamole and fish tacos."

He turned and pulled her along, running down the paved street.

Today was her day, and he wanted to generate a new memory—one she would never forget.

Her giggle floated around them and fizzed with tiny bubbles of happiness.

However much he wanted to throw her in a cab and take her back to his place, he'd wait—wait until she was ready.

Today she might not know who she wanted to be, but he sure hoped she didn't mind him bumming a ride while she traveled the road of discovery.

Chapter Thirteen

Jacob promised a day filled with fun and laughter, and he delivered.

Not once during the day did she feel uncomfortable, until the taxi proceeded through the massive security gate and up the winding road to the top of the vista overlooking the city. The cab pulled in front of a buttercup stucco building with a Spanish-style roof and wrought iron accents.

She grabbed her purse and slid out of the back seat. He lent her a hand and helped her to the curb.

The red front door was a bit of a surprise, but the cream marble flooring, vaulted ceiling, and battleship grey walls weren't. She had nailed his taste with a capital T.

He lived simply.

He stuck to a palette of only a few colors, with one bold, accenting color to highlight something within each space, like the red door.

He tossed his keys on the counter and moved their suitcases around the corner to remove the tripping hazard. Next, he opened the sliding door to a deck overlooking the city lights below to let in the fresh breeze.

"I'm in the mood for chardonnay. Would you like a glass?"

She nodded and walked toward the deck, rubbing her arms to ward off an anxious chill. She felt trapped. Jacob might not have meant to, but he'd put her in another cage. The claustrophobia pressed in, and she became preoccupied with what came next.

What would he expect? Sex? Friendship? People always had a way of making demands on others, whether intended or not.

"I love seeing the city lights from here." He handed her a glass of white wine. "I realized just now, I should have asked whether you want to stay here. I was too wrapped up in the presentation to plan anything beyond the meeting."

She looked through the glass at the floor-to-ceiling grey rock fireplace, the large screen television with a game console underneath, and a cozy living room area. She couldn't see his bedroom, but assumed it was upstairs. Out of sight, out of mind...for now. The sizeable cream-colored couch could be an option.

"It's uncomfortable. You'll get a crick in your neck, and will be cranky come morning."

"I'm sorry?" She asked, doing her best to figure out what he meant.

He pointed. "The couch. You were thinking about sleeping on the couch, weren't you?" He fought off the smile, but in the end he lost. "There is a guest room. It's just off the kitchen. You will be perfectly safe there."

Safe. Yes. Most of her life she'd been cautious, watching what she said, how she presented herself, what she did. She played the part her father wanted her to play perfectly. She didn't want to be perfect anymore.

"Thanks. I'll sleep there."

Disappointment settled across his face, but he didn't add pressure, only accepted her decision.

"I've been in this suit all day. I don't know about you, but I want to change into something more...comfortable."

First, he untucked his business shirt from his trousers. A suit guy he wasn't. His coat and tie had long ago disappeared. Peeking through the blue cotton, his tanned skin beckoned her to touch. His fingers moved from button to button. With each passing second, she consciously suppressed the urge to lick her lips.

He was gorgeous, his skin smooth and sweet as warm honey. Saliva pooled with her need to touch, to kiss.

"I'll wait." She placed her wine glass on the deck table to keep from dropping the glass, and crossed her arms. "You go ahead."

"You sure?"

"We had an agreement, remember?"

He took a step closer. "No innuendos. No kisses. No massages. And certainly no sex," he repeated. "But, if you remember, my agreement lasts only until you acknowledge the connection we have. You decide the next step." He smiled. "But you asked me to kiss you once. Would you like another?"

"No. I'm good."

Yes, his bronzed skin beckoned her to touch. To slide her fingers along the delicate hair disappearing below his belt. "Then again, I'm not so sure."

He moved a little closer, letting his mouth hover over her lips. "Kiss me, Rachelle."

Her lips seized his. He pressed deeper. His mouth was needy. Demanding. She could feel the heat from his torso soaking through her shirt. Her hands slid up and over his shoulders, and she wrapped her arms around his neck. Damn. Her whole body homed in on him, lifting, tightening, craving more.

Then he was gone.

Darn her heart for lamenting the loss.

"I'm not doing this. I'm not playing fair. I want you, Rachelle, but I promised. You need to decide." He held his hands splayed in front of him and backed up slowly. "This is your day." He loosened his belt. Her eyes followed his happy trail that lead to... "Are those Spiderman briefs?"

He looked down, and his cheeks turned a bit pink. "Don't tell me. You'd prefer Superman."

"No. Spiderman's fine. I mean he's sort of the

underdog of all superheroes. He's sensitive, reliable, and a bit nerdy...in a cute, sexy way."

"Don't forget he swings from buildings and swoops in to save damsels in distress." The heat from his whispered reminder sent shivers down her spine.

"Spiderman does like to play the hero. Although he is a bit on the serious side."

His eyes grew darker, more intent. "Do you want to play?"

"Maybe some other time."

He stepped back. "I'll go take a shower. If you change your mind and want to play rub-a-dub-dub, you're always welcome."

He disappeared through the doorway, only to reappear a second later behind the glass window. He sauntered through his living room without a care. He was comfortable here. Funny enough, so was she. She stepped off the deck into the kitchen to pick up her luggage. After a few seconds, she found the spare room and shower, as promised.

When she turned on the light, she gasped.

The entire room was full of floor to ceiling bookcases littered with miniature action figure collections from comic books, movies, and games, each six-inch collection methodically stored on a four-tiered plastic shelf.

On the next shelf, comic books in plastic sleeves were carefully stacked. A shadow box drew her closer. A book. She didn't recognize the author or title, but the pages were curled from so many readings. The image of him sitting at his mother's side reading came fluttering back, and she'd bet a lot of money his mother had given his precious keepsake.

She inhaled a deep breath and closed the bedroom door, for no other reason than to avoid the temptation named Jacob Reyes, who was showering upstairs. He was a study in contrasts. A man, yet a boy wanting to be loved.

The old Rachelle would have followed him up the

stairs without thought. The new Rachelle needed to think.

What did she want?

She studied her image in the mirror with horror. There was a slight sunburn line around the left side of her face where she'd missed when applying her SPF moisturizer. Her hair was a mess. Her blouse had sweat and grease stains from where a piece of fish fell out of her taco. She lifted a hand to smooth her brows, but instead she dropped her hand to the counter.

Who was the person staring back in the mirror? She didn't know. Who was this woman? What did she want? The only thing she felt was confused, jumbled.

She'd worked so hard to put her shattered life back together, but finding all the millions of scattered pieces was a daunting task.

Determination bullied its way in.

She would put her life back together. But what did she want her life to look like? Could she accept help? Should she?

She bent to turn the shower on, then reached for a rag to remove her makeup. One layer at a time, she scrubbed and scrubbed and scrubbed until the layers disappeared.

She rotated her head examining her face, first the left side, then right. "Hm. Not bad."

She no longer needed to be perfect. Look perfect. Flawed could be her new perfect.

Her future was about trying and failing and trying something new.

Stepping into the shower, she let the water cascade down her body, washing away the years of isolation, mental anguish, abuse.

She was free to choose.

The only problem? She didn't have a clue what came next.

Chapter Fourteen

Jacob lay sprawled on his bed, his forearm over his eyes.

She didn't trust him. Not just him. She didn't trust anyone.

She hid it well. Earlier in the day, he could see the way her hands bunched into fists as soon as the investors walked into the room. She smiled, her shoulders were relaxed, but her hands were white knuckleballs. At the pier, she moved behind him, using him as a barrier, when a guy needing change approached.

She didn't need to fear him.

He would never do anything she didn't want him to, but he didn't have a clue how to open the doors and get past her reticence.

A sound coming from the hall shifted his attention. He held his breath to still his heartbeat.

"Don't go," he called into the darkness.

"I didn't know if you were still awake." Rachelle's darkened profile appeared in the doorway.

How could I not? You consume me. "Do you need something?" *Please, say me.*

"I...um...no. I'm good. I just wanted to say thanks."

"For?" he slowly lifted into a seated position. "I'm the one who dragged you to California to help me with my presentation."

"For today. For showing me the city." She took a few more tentative steps toward the bed. He barely breathed. One flinch and she'd be down the stairs and locked away in a flash.

"I had fun."

She took another step closer. The moonbeam from the skylight above his bed set her in a spotlight. He could see every luscious curve. The sheer joy of seeing her standing in his room caused all his body parts to switch to party mode. His groin tensed when she took another tentative step closer.

A whiff of her floral shampoo quietly filled the room. He closed his eyes and took in her essence. His fingers itched to reach out and touch her, but he remained still and focused on his breathing.

He opened his eyes to see her next to the bed. "Why are you here Rachelle?"

"I don't know."

He adjusted the sheets at his waist. "Then perhaps you'd better go back downstairs. I want you in the worst way, and the longer you stand there, the more I want you. But you need to know why you're here first."

She didn't leave—halleluiah. In fact, her chest heaved with indecision.

"It's odd. Before...I mean, when my dad controlled my life, I rebelled by pretending I was a seductress. The men in my father's world wanted to be teased, then caught. I learned to perform the part my father had assigned, and perfected it over the years."

Bile soured his throat, his fists bunched the bedding, and he closed his eyes to swallow the disgust. "I don't want you to be, or do, anything you don't want to, Rachelle."

"I know." She glanced back at the door, then surprised him by inching closer. "It's just I don't know what to do when I'm not playing a role. You're right. I feel the connection with you, but I'm not sure what to do about how I feel without giving you the wrong impression."

"Come here." He turned back the comforter and sheets. "Let me hold you for a while."

She knelt on the bed, then snuggled in next to him. He

wrapped his body slowly around hers, careful not to trap her in any way. "Comfortable?"

"I feel you."

"Yes, well, I can't help it. My body is making it clear it wants you."

He leaned closer to take in her smell, then settled his head on the pillow, although he knew in about twenty minutes he wouldn't be able to feel his arm. But he didn't care. She was with him. That's what mattered.

He tightened his arm to adjust and feel the maximum skin possible, conforming to the lines of her body perfectly. There wasn't one gap. Her hair splayed on his pillow felt so natural. So...right.

"Jacob?"

"Uh-huh?"

She traced a finger down his forearm. "I think our bodies are communicating with each other."

His eyes opened wider, his breath becoming a bit faster. "And what are they saying?"

"Please."

He brushed the hair from her face. "I told you before...it's up to you to decide."

"I can't."

"Yes you can. You already know what you want. At least I believe your body knows." He shifted onto his elbow to search her face. "Your dad isn't here. You," he kissed her temple, "you get to choose."

She rolled onto her back. "Will you help me?"

"Always," he whispered against her lips. Her feather light touch teased and slid along his torso, then she shifted, throwing a leg over his thigh. When he hissed, she giggled, and her hands became more animated.

His muscles tightened as he tried to remain still, but every cell wanted to connect, to fuse with her. She straddled him, then lifted the hem of her nightshirt, the moon creating shadows in many of her erotic places. She dropped little kisses on his chest.

He reached up and traced the side of her breast with his fingertips, then circled her nipples until the skin puckered. After a few minutes, his hands drifted lower, and he reached for her core.

"Not yet." She scooted back.

He playfully caught her wrist. "Do you want to see me beg?" He placed her fingers in his mouth and sucked, caressing her skin with his tongue.

"Spiderman doesn't beg."

He sat up and held her in his lap, leaning in, giving her breasts the same treatment as her fingers. She threw back her head, groaned, and arched her back, her body begging for more while one of his hands dallied lower to find the right spot and the other drew her closer. He wanted her to scream his name when her body pulsed with pleasure.

"Jacob, there. Yes, there."

He adjusted the speed and pressure based on her response. She undulated on top of him and sent electrical pulses surging through his body, her thighs gripping his like a clamp.

"Talk to me."

"More. Yes." She arched back, her mouth slack. He'd never seen a piece of human art more beautiful. He wanted to make her remember this moment—the exact second she no longer had to play a role. The day she got to be the one whose needs were fulfilled. He wanted to give her this.

He nipped playfully at her breasts.

"Yes. Do that again," she sighed.

Her fingers wove into his hair, then let his tongue and fingers work their magic.

Until it happened—she screamed his name into the room, then collapsed against him.

Enjoying the rise and fall of her breath, he brushed a hand slowly up and down her back.

"Wow. So that's what an orgasm is supposed to feel

like."

He brushed the hair from her face. "Are you telling me—?"

"—I told you before, men are selfish, self-centered bastards."

He reached up and cupped her chin, stroking a thumb across her jawline. "And I told you I'm not like other men."

"I know."

He rolled her to his side, but she nudged him back. "Please tell me you're not tired."

Of you? Never. "What do you have in mind?"

"Let me show you."

Chapter Fifteen

Rachelle tucked her cold toes into the hem of Jacob's sweatpants and reached for her coffee. The morning sun had just reached the deck, but hadn't yet had the chance to warm the air.

She savored the lingering rich, bitter swallow of dark roast and almond. She hadn't had a decent cup for months and was taking full advantage of freshly ground coffee and a state-of-the-art brewer...even though she would never take advantage of the coffee's owner.

He was the kind of guy who liked to take care of people. She could tell.

Letting him take care of her would be easy—too easy—but she couldn't. After a while she'd resent him, and hate herself for the very thing she allowed him to do.

She'd learned how to survive. Now she needed to learn how to live on her own.

Yesterday was a thrill. The look on the investors' faces when she presented her art. They liked it. No, they loved what she had created.

Maybe she could do her art by night and interior design by day.

The patio door opened. "Please tell me there's more coffee."

He sounded like an old lawnmower cranking and sputtering before turning over. He leaned in and kissed her forehead before settling on the opposite chair.

"I made a full pot." She slid a mug and the thermos his direction, knowing he liked his coffee black.

He pointed. "I was wondering where my sweatpants ran off to."

"Do you mind?"

"Nope." He settled back in the chair and looked out over the horizon.

She held up her cell phone with a picture of Dempsey playing with a tug-toy. "You were right. Dempsey is having fun at the kennel. Yesterday Karly sent me a short video of him running around with a pit bull."

"Do you miss him?"

Miss him? The question jerked her emotions. "I've never been a dog person, but yeah, I miss him." The tension she wasn't aware she was holding eased. "He takes up a lot of my time, but he's become my little buddy."

"Speaking of time, we've got a busy day."

The thread of calm she was trying to braid together snapped. "We do?"

"I want us to meet my design team."

I was hoping you'd change your mind.

This wasn't good. Another man tucking her neatly into his life. She couldn't go there. Not yet. She needed to learn who she was first.

"That's what you said, but meeting the team may not be a good idea. You saw how Larson reacted." She stretched her sweater over her hands and curled tightly into the chair. "Why don't you go and meet with your team? I don't mind hanging out here." On the street below a couple of kids rolled by on skateboards, and gave her another idea. "I could help Ben. He said he needed help. After I've showered, I'll give him a call."

I'll volunteer to do anything to avoid spending the day with you. You rattle my brain, not to mention the delicious things you do to my body parts.

He shook his head. "Ben texted me this morning. He's already delegated the tasks and fully implemented your plan. He said to let you know everything is under control."

She smiled back at him, not knowing what to say. She shifted uneasily in the chair.

Over his cup, he watched her for a moment, then set the mug on the table and reached for her hand. "Talk to me."

Her old self would have made excuses, told him everything was fine, or feigned innocence. He was the most amazing man she'd ever met, and she wasn't about to let him take on her demons. She needed to learn how to become the person she wanted to be. To grow, she needed space and time.

Why did life have to be unpredictable?

Fate's timing sucked.

Jacob got up from his chair, walked two steps, then swooped her into his arms.

She clutched her coffee to her torso. "What are you doing?"

He sat down in her Adirondack chair. "There. That's better. You were too far away." He tightened his grip to ensure she wouldn't fall. "I bet I know what you're thinking."

"How could you know?" she pressed a hand against his chest, but he held her tight.

"Just let me hold you. I'll let you go in a minute." He reached for his coffee cup and took a sip. "First I want you to tell me why you're scared."

She gasped softly, her eyes wide. "Why would you think I'm scared?" She set her coffee on the table, no longer wanting to add more bitterness to her already churning stomach.

He whispered into her ear. "You always clench your fist when you get scared."

She opened her fingers and pressed them flat against her thighs. "You're too observant for your own good, Mr. Reyes."

"It comes from studying the way humans move. The goal is to create realism in my games."

He gently nudged her with his shoulder. "Now, will you tell me what's wrong, or will I have to take you down and dump you in my pool and not let you out until you tell me?"

"You wouldn't."

He leaned forward, and she was up and over his shoulder in a matter of seconds as he walked inside the house.

"Put me down." Fear choked off her air. She beat his back with her fists. "Stop. Put me down." Petrified of what was coming next, she froze.

Noooooo. The room grew hazy.

She blinked, and blinked again.

Her hair dangled in front of her face.

She let it fall.

A high-pitched whimper, echoed in her head.

She blinked, trying to focus.

His muscles went slack, and her body shifted. A chill registered when her feet touched the tile.

Her body began to vibrate.

Her mind turned inward.

Warm hands tugged her stiff arms away from her chest.

"Jeezus, Rachelle." Jacob took a couple of steps back, his hand up, fingers splayed, out of her safety zone. "I'm sorry. I should have known."

Shivers sent goose bumps skidding around her skin. Her fury erupted as rage consumed her. Adrenaline pulses of outrage shot through every vein.

"Should have known what?" She staggered forward, and shoved him back. "That I'm broken. That I'm screwed up? That I don't know who I am?"

"I was playing, and I crossed the line." He sank down on the leather couch and looked up at her. "I'm not the bad guy here. Your father," he rubbed his palms down his legs, "he's the one who should have protected you. Instead he hurt you." His knees bounced, going faster and faster. "You don't know me yet, but you will. And when you do, you'll understand I'm trying to build something good here. Okay? I didn't mean to scare you."

"No, it's not okay." She paced away, then back. "You can't fix me, just like you can't fix Larson. You think you can, but you can't. Each of us, Larson and I, we're the ones who need to fix what's wrong. Not you."

He thumped a fist on his thigh. "What about last night? Did you think I was trying to fix you then?"

"No. Last night...last night was beautiful. It was the first time I felt real. I was me, not the idea of who someone else wanted me to be."

"Then tell me how I'm trying to fix you."

"By giving me a job. Paying for my storyboards. By flying me here."

He was up and around the coffee table in two steps. "I didn't hire you, Ben did. And he hired you based on your qualifications and talents. He made a good hiring decision. Your designs are first rate.

"Secondly, I pay my top designers a lot more for their storyboards. I offered you half, just to see what you came up with. And I flew you here, not because I felt sorry for you, but because I needed your support in the investor meeting. The investors are careful. They don't want any copyright challenges. I anticipated them wanting to know where the ideas came from. Who better to answer the questions than the person who came up with them?"

He took a few steps closer. "Tell me again how I'm trying to fix you."

She turned her head to avoid the intensity in his generous eyes. "You're not."

"Say it like you mean it." His voice sounded sharp, but she wasn't afraid. He wouldn't force her to do anything she didn't want to do.

"I'm sorry."

"No." He raked his fingers through his hair. "I don't want you to be sorry. I want you to be right. I want to hear the conviction in your voice, like when you know a room is designed perfectly. I want you to believe in yourself. No matter what, I want you to know your opinion is the right one."

"I'm getting there."

"Good. That's good." He kept getting closer and closer. He licked his lips, his focus on her intensifying. "You're a beautiful woman, Rachelle, and when I say beautiful, I mean in here." He pointed at his chest.

She reached out a tentative hand and pressed her palm on his skin, letting the beat of his heart pulse into her hand. "You're the first person who's ever taken the time to see me."

He covered her hand with his, holding it in place until their bodies eased into a synchronized rhythm. "Now that we set some boundaries"—he pressed the tip of his nose to hers and studied her eyes—"let's get dressed and go get some grub. I'm hungry."

"Now?"

"Now." He kissed her nose, then walked toward the kitchen, while scratching his butt cheek, his shorts fabric bunching with every swipe.

"That's it? Just like that, all's forgiven?"

"Unless you want to talk more." He shrugged. "It's a guy thing. What can I say? Life is too short to keep regurgitating things. Besides, I told you, I'm not like anyone you've ever met before." He walked back toward her, rubbing his head. "Now go change before I decide to eat you for breakfast."

"Breakfast?" She moved a few tentative steps closer. "How about another one of your amazing kisses?"

"Oh, God. Don't look at me like that."

She slipped her fingers into the tops of his waistband and tugged. "Why?" she laughed, rotated, then backed toward the kitchen island. "You said you wanted breakfast."

His eyes snapped open, and he snagged her so fast she

didn't have time to take a breath. "Woman, you're killing me." His arms wrapped around her, then loosened. "Get upstairs and take my sweatpants off...now."

"No."

Automatically he released her, but she tugged him back.

His eyes darkened, and he bit his lip. "Remember, I'm just a simple guy. Tell me what you want."

"Jacob." She crooked a finger in his underwear band. "Now, please."

"Got it." He backed her against the refrigerator. "One hot breakfast, coming up."

Chapter Sixteen

Jacob parallel-parked his Mercedes C 63 along the busy urban street.

Rachelle grabbed her purse and waited while Jacob fed the parking meter. Her shoulders screamed with jittery tension. She shouldn't be nervous. Her father had taken her to hundreds of business meetings. But instinct told her this meeting would be vastly different. Jacob wanted her to get involved.

With her permission, Jacob had sent his team her drawings.

What would they think? They were the experts. Not her.

"Did you hear back from Larson?"

"Not yet. Relax. Everything will be fine. The team is going to love you. You're creative. You speak the same language."

"Lines and lighting and color selection aren't exactly a language."

"Tell that to Drew, Sketch, and Etch," He chuckled, and she didn't get exactly why. "Half the time I have no idea what they're talking about."

"Those are nicknames, right?"

"Not all. Drew Caster is the lead game designer, and his actual name is Drew. He nicknamed Sketch and Etch, since the three of them work in tandem designing the game architecture. Where there's one, you can usually find all three huddled together."

Just great. She'd watched close-knit groups work,

oblivious to everything outside their micro-universe, and rarely letting outsiders join their circle.

"When you say they're game architects, what does that mean exactly?"

"In each level, a programmer places objects and triggers in place for the gamer to find and use. Some objects are put there to confuse the player. Others are used to solve the clues. Some items the player will need to pick up—like a scroll or weapon. These types of items will be used for solving or getting access to other layers. Game architecture takes time and planning, and the design team usually grows close as a result."

"Sorry, I still don't get it."

"Okay." He turned and walked backwards. "Think of a house with a whole bunch of rooms. Each house is decorated differently. In each room, there is a key you need to find, or an activity to complete before you can enter the next room."

He must have seen the light bulb flicker on, because he took her hand, and faced the direction they were walking again. "The designers create everything from the room to the objects in the room to the characters. Once the designs are finished, they turn the designs over to the animators, who bring their visions to life."

"Let me see if I've got this straight. You develop the story, the designers create an environment to support your story, and the animators computerize the information to put the pieces together."

"There's a lot of back and forth, but that's pretty much it." His smile reminded her of her brother's when he was successful in explaining to their father how his complex science project worked.

"Here we are." He stopped at the café's entrance and held the large wooden door open for her. At a table on the deck overlooking the beach, a tall, thin man stood and shoved a pair of sunglasses to the top of his head. He wore a black T-shirt that read, "Just assume I'm never wrong."

He fist-knocked Jacob on the shoulder. "Good to see you, man."

"You, too. Hey, Drew, this is Rachelle."

Drew did a quick scan of Jacob's hand on her lower back. Eventually his gaze managed to make its way to her face. "Rachelle. Jacob says you have some ideas for the new game."

She adjusted the purse on her shoulder and shifted uneasily. "I just painted a few blocks to support his presentation."

"Is she for real?" Drew asked, laughing.

Before Rachelle could figure out what Drew meant, a tall brunette with a teal-colored Mohawk punched Drew in the arm. "Be nice." She extended her hand. "I'm Sketch, and what this geek is trying to say is, your drawings are sweeeeet." She pointed a thumb over her shoulder. "That's Etch. Don't mind her. She's got her G-string all twisted this morning."

Jacob's forehead lined with concern. "What's up with her?"

Etch's thumbs moved at lightning speed over her phone screen. With each pause, her frown deepened.

"Larson." Sketch dragged the two syllables through the mud. Etch's follow-up expression communicated a lot, only Rachelle couldn't interpret the message.

Jacob walked around the table. "Etch. Tell me."

The petite woman with short black hair and a buzzed lightning rod design on one side paused her texting long enough to hit Jacob with a look. "We were supposed to test the equipment for tomorrow's gig, but Larson's adding another last-minute feature for the kids. He's got the source code locked, though, so we can't compile the game."

"What's he doing?" Jacob turned to Drew for answers.

"Don't look at me, man. He's your problem. You're the only one he listens to."

"Where is he now?" Jacob looked at Etch, his brow rising in question.

Etch shrugged. "He's not saying, but he's not at the office or home. We checked both places before we got here."

Jacob slid out a chair and turned to Rachelle. "I'm starved. Let's have breakfast." Jacob winked at her, and her cheeks heated, knowing Jacob never got his eggs or pancakes for breakfast. He got her instead. "I'll deal with Larson later."

Drew, Sketch, and Etch looked at each other in turn. Something was up, but she couldn't read the intense body language. She gave up and sat in the seat Jacob held for her. He leaned close to her eye. "Relax."

Relax? Jacob should take his own advice. If he'd been a cat, he'd be a fluff ball, walking sideways and hissing.

Drew handed her a menu. "We always order the same things when we come here."

"Do you have a recommendation?"

"Any of the fresh-squeezed juices or egg dishes. Everything is made fresh. You can't go wrong."

Thankful for something to do, she studied the menu like she'd have a pop quiz any second. The conversation swirled around her and became background noise until she realized the sound had stopped.

She lowered the menu to see Sketch's genuine interest. "What did I miss?"

Jacob reached and squeezed her hand underneath the table.

"We were talking about the new game," Sketch placed her elbows on the table. "I want to hear your idea."

"Well, I..." She choked on the fear. Would they like the idea? With her father, she could anticipate the nuances of his moods. She could calculate when to push, hold, and fold. Here she wasn't sure how to play the game, and had no idea of the stakes.

Now she was in uncharted territory. So she donned

her easy-to-wear princess's persona and proceeded. "Based on Jacob's story, I developed a few sample landscapes. After he chose a couple, I created some characters to fit the world. Everything can be changed. It's not like the investors were looking for the story to be final. They just wanted to know the concept."

"Just a few landscapes, she says," Sketch shoved her silverware set aside. "Best damn ideas we've ever seen in over a year, and she acts like she just pulled them out of her butt."

Etch twisted her phone around, "This one." The rainforest appeared vivid and sharp on the tiny screen. "Why did you choose a pyramid and not a dome shape to protect the city?"

Rachelle gulped down a wad of nerves. "Triangles made sense. I was thinking about energy, and how it needs to build to a fine point before being distributed. I've seen domes in drawings, but they've never made sense. I read somewhere the pyramids in Egypt were based on some ancient engineering design given to the human race by the aliens to be used to transfer energy."

"You believe that shit?" Drew's skepticism skipped across the table.

"No, I don't, but it doesn't matter what I believe. Helping Jacob meet his deadline—that's what mattered. I didn't think, I just painted what I thought would work to support his story."

"In other words, you pulled the design out of your butt."

Rachelle narrowed her eyes at the too-serious woman. "I'd like to think I pulled the images out of my head, but sure."

Jacob rested an arm on the back of her chair and chuckled. "Well done. I don't think I've ever seen a speechless Sketch."

Etch shoved her phone forward again and pointed. "What about the waterfall?"

The groans rounded the table, and Etch blushed the shade of a peony petal.

"Etch's question is intuitive." Rachelle paused to get everyone's attention. "I put in the waterfall because water is a conductor of electricity, and the water could be another way to protect the city."

A grateful smirk replaced Etch's curious expression.

A hush fell over the table.

Drew pointed a finger. "Please tell me she's under contract."

Jacob shifted in his chair. "I haven't asked her yet."

"Dude, what are you waiting for? You better lock her solid before someone else finds out how good she is."

Good? Rachelle crossed her legs beneath the chair. He thought she was good?

"I've been telling you your work is amazing."

Amazing? The expressions on their faces were almost identical. A sizzle of satisfaction danced around and did a pirouette in her heart. They liked her work.

"Ready to order breakfast?" A cute blonde approached the table, and everyone got down to ordering.

"Etch," Drew tossed a piece of wadded-up paper at his buddy. "What's percolating?"

She reached into her pocket, then grabbed the nearest napkin. Big, sweeping lines were followed by small details, and within minutes a female clad in armor appeared. The busty, narrow-waisted vixen looked so typical, Rachelle groaned inwardly. She'd seen the same things hundreds of time.

There was no originality.

No uniqueness.

Just the same old idea, circling the drain again and again.

She sat back in her chair and watched while the napkin was thoroughly inspected, then passed again.

Jacob squeezed her knee, "What do you think?"

"It's nice." Rachelle passed the napkin to Drew.

Jacob's gaze snapped to hers and locked on, his eyes narrowing. "Talk to me."

Her jaw tightened. She shook her head slightly and looked away to avoid the spotlight.

"Etch," Jacob said. "Can I borrow your pen?" Without hesitation, she tossed the pen across the table. Jacob placed the pen and his napkin in front of Rachelle with a dare-you brow lift.

She gripped the edge of the table, then her right arm slowly reached for the pen and she let her gut instincts pour out the tip. The vision of a female warrior with armor designed to intimidate yet defend emerged on the white. A mixture of Norse and Celtic. Of strength, yet feminine. There wasn't anything sexual about the character. She was simply strong and in control of her world.

Rachelle set the pen down, her hands sliding back into her lap.

Jacob picked up the napkin and turned it around for everyone at the table to see. Etch held out her hand with her fingers wiggling. Jacob gave the drawing and pen to Sketch, who passed it along.

Etch scratched her head, then stared off into a distance.

Etch popped the lid off the pen. "May I?" The pen hovered over the napkin.

"Sure," Rachelle responded.

Within a few swipes of the pen, weapons appeared. If Rachelle hadn't drawn the warrior, she wouldn't be able to tell where her lines ended and Etch's began.

A feeling of camaraderie sent shivers up her arms, and the fine hairs on her arms stood up to celebrate. Belonging. Being part of something big filled her soul. She hadn't known how empty she was until this moment. She studied each person at the table, memorizing their smiles, friendly expressions, and creative camaraderie they'd shown her. She'd remember every nuance.

Etch finished and held up the revised drawing.

"Now, that's what I call one kick-ass bitch. I wouldn't mess with her," Etch let a smile slip into place.

"I'll get her digi'd," Drew added.

Sketch grabbed the napkin. "You got your peacock."

Jacob shifted and faked a cough. "Yo, Earth Gamers."

"Oh, sorry, boss." Sketch turned to Jacob. "Etch has wanted to design a female with peacock coloring; you know purples, greens, blues. We just never had a design that worked until now." Her pupils dilated with excitement. "Give Etch twenty-four hours, and she'll have a model we can play with."

"I keep telling you, man." Drew pointed. "You'd better get Rach signed up, fast. We need her on the team."

"Well, how about it?" The look on Jacob's face was hopeful.

She'd get to draw, create every day. How cool was that?

Something in her held back.

Designing games. Was this the career path she was meant to follow? And what about Jacob?

He had expectations.

Should she get in a relationship now, when she was still trying to figure things out? Was pleasing him the only reason she thought about accepting the job? What about her needs? She'd lose herself in the relationship. Jacob could be all-consuming. If she didn't take the time to figure out who she wanted to be, instinct told her she'd never get another chance.

The praise heated the nape of her neck. "I a...I need to think about it?"

"What's there to think about?" Sketch's expression was curious, but there was a little dose of tension in the question.

Good thing the waitress arrived with platefuls of food to flick off the spotlight. She needed to come up with an answer. Fast.

When everyone settled again, Jacob picked up his fork and turned to her. "You don't want to be part of the design team?"

"I'd love to, but there are a few things back home I need to settle first. I'll help any way I can, but I need you to give me some time."

Drew shoved a wad of omelet in his mouth. "Give her a month," he mumbled around the eggs, spinach, and feta.

"A month?" Etch shook her head. "A week."

"How about split the difference. Two weeks." Sketch winked at Rachelle.

"Guys." Jacob's hand caressing her knee beneath the table felt incredibly good, so good she forgot to chew. "This is Rachelle's decision. Let's give her some time." A slow smile crept across his mouth, and he got the look she'd seen before in his eyes. "How about we give her until the end of the day?" He twirled the fork in his hand over the back of his thumb and caught it again. "Just kidding." He laughed.

Everyone at the table joined in, even her.

Hiking to the top of the mountain and looking out over the vast vistas of the Rockies couldn't feel better than this moment did.

She felt needed, wanted, for the first time in years.

The feeling was addictive.

If only she could say yes.

Chapter Seventeen

Jacob stood on his back deck and let the soft breeze from the ocean cool his skin. Unfortunately, the sparkling stars didn't stop his aching erection from reminding him how much he wanted Rachelle.

After the lunch meeting she became quiet, distant. They spent hours walking along the Imperial Beach pier, watching the waves crash into the white sand and beach lovers enjoying the sun. Rachelle offered some sporadic conversation about people, places, and dreams, but she'd been distracted, deep into her head.

He hadn't. He'd been paying close attention— watching each change of expression.

Watching the moon, he could still remember the sun streaming down on her blond curls, her skin turning pink in the sun, her glorious smile. He loved experiencing her childlike need to indulge in sugar-coated nuts, collect seashells, and sit on a rock to watch kites fly. Unearthing each nuance made him want to spend more time with her.

After taking a shower, he went down to check on her and found her sprawled facedown on her bed asleep. If he touched her, she would respond to the inevitable. His body belonged to her. And she responded to his need. He could have awakened her with a stroke on her arm or a light kiss on her forehead, but then she might have assumed he just wanted sex.

He didn't just want sex. He wanted her heart, yet she would only give him what she thought he wanted. If she only had an inkling how much he simply wanted her in his life. She colored his black and white world and made him want things he hadn't known were absent until she came along.

He had seen her hesitation—the pain in her eyes reminding him her past still chained her heart.

Time. It would take time for her to realize he wouldn't do anything to jeopardize—

Arms wrapped around his waist, inviting his thoughts to indulge in her warmth.

"I fell asleep."

Her voice was soft, gentle against the quiet of the night.

"There were so many things I wanted to show you. I overdid it a little today."

Her laughter vibrated against his skin. "It was a nonstop day. My feet couldn't take any more walking."

"You said you didn't know the real me. I wanted to show you the places I love and let you experience the real geek."

"I like the geek." Her fingers slid across his chest, and she tightened her hold, placing sweet kisses on his back. "It's the most fun I've ever had."

"The most fun?" He closed his eyes to indulge in the incredible feeling.

"The most fun. If I bundled up all the fun I ever had before today, it still wouldn't have come close."

He turned and touched her bare arm.

Bad move. Seeing her pink T-shirt and white lace panties erected a tent in his nylon shorts and fired up his groin. He ignored his aching need and smoothed back her hair, then cupped her sweet, adorable face.

"We're good together—you and I."

She laid her head on his chest, released a long sigh, and tightened her arms around his back. Her form pressed and molded against his body. He could feel her nipples, hard and pointed, wanting attention.

Instinctively, he wrapped his arms around her, shielding her from the early morning air. Her warm breath skidded across the surface of his skin. He lifted the back of her shirt, letting his fingers cruise across her skin.

"You're getting cold. I feel goose bumps."

She dragged her teeth across his nipple.

He gasped.

"I'm not cold." Her voice sounded sensual, aroused.

"God, woman, how I want you," he whispered, pulling her tight against his erection. "Can't you tell?"

"What are you going to do about it?"

He clenched his teeth, then eased his jaw muscles. "Nothing," he whispered, then leaned back and kissed her forehead. "I told you before. What happens between us is your decision."

However, his hands had different ideas. His fingers slid around her sides, across her skin to caress her breasts. For a second, she didn't move, then dropped her head back, thrusting her enticing softness against him, shoulders to knees. He closed his eyes, letting his fingers see and feel the slope and lines of her body.

He pressed his groin against her again to make sure she understood his need. He wanted her. Needed her.

"What if I demanded you take me—any way you want—right now?"

He squeezed her breast, unable to control his reaction. "I'd have to think about your motives. Is domination what you truly want? Or is it the only thing you know?"

She drew a line down his torso with her fingertip. "Before I was always the one in control. I never trusted anyone."

He slipped his hand underneath the elastic of her panties to touch her sweet spot. "Is this truly what you want?"

"Yes."

The immediate response gave him a jolt. He let his fingers play. "What else?"

"That's for you to decide," she replied in a sultry whisper, all the while dragging her hands over his lower abs to dip in and out of his waistband.

He closed his eyes and hissed when her fingers touched him and made him jerk his eyes open. She withdrew the pressure. His engorged hard-on begged for her fingers to explore, stroke, love.

She moaned, and he leaned in to suck on her neck.

"I want you, Jacob. I want this. But only with you."

He yanked her to him, hard. And there it was, the fear she couldn't hide.

"You don't trust me yet."

"It's not you." She turned to look out at the horizon. "I don't want to be scared anymore. I need to put my past behind me. It's just..."

"Can you talk about what happened?"

She coiled inward, crossing her arms, shutting him out. "No." She reached for his arm. "Please understand. I need to protect you."

"Me?" *What the hell?* Understanding began to surface. "Your dad. He didn't—"

"No." Her grip tightened. "No, but there are still some loose ends with my dad. If I tell you, you'll be involved, and I don't want anyone I care about tainted by my father."

She cares about me.

Then she refused to meet his gaze, looking down and rolling her feet to the outside edges, biting her lip.

A welling of hatred for the men who made this beautiful and strong and glorious woman into a wounded bird made him want to break something.

"Your father's in jail. He can't hurt you anymore."

She shook her head.

"He's not in jail?"

When she looked at him, her eyes were shimmering with tears. "My father is in jail, but he has connections on the outside. There are powerful men connected to him who are still free. If I do what my dad wants, I'll be okay."

"He wants to control you, even from behind bars."

The thought of someone hurting her made him break out in a sweat. "I promise you, Rachelle, if anyone—and I mean anyone—tries to hurt you, I'll make sure they never walk again."

"No. See, that's why I can't let you get involved. These men...no, I can't talk about this."

"Yes you can. You can tell me, and I'll make sure nothing happens to you."

"Please, Jacob." She shook her head and started backing away.

He reached for her hand. "Don't. Don't shut me out." But she already had. Until she felt safe—she wouldn't be able to be with him fully.

The wind picked up and blew through her hair, lifting the tender ends. She was so strong, yet so fragile. Until she was able to box the hurt and fear and store it away, she would forever guard her heart. Her father would always be there, preventing·her from living the life she deserved.

A heavy sigh released some of the hormones romping through his system. "Rachelle. Look at me."

Her eyes slowly lifted to meet his, and she brushed away the tears.

"I'm not going anywhere." He ran his knuckles down her cheek. "Every time you look around, I'll be here to support you." He put an arm around her shoulder. "Let's go in. You're getting cold."

She nodded, and they slowly made their way inside.

After he closed the door, he turned toward the couch.

She hesitated. "We're not going upstairs?"

"In about an hour the sun will rise. I thought we could watch it together, unless you would rather sleep."

"But your charity event is this afternoon."

He nodded. "I wouldn't be able to sleep anyway. What do you say? Will you stay with me?"

Chapter Eighteen

Jacob brought Rachelle a throw from the hall closet, then went to heat some water for the herbal tea she bought at one of the many booths they passed during the day.

She burrowed under the throw, doing her best to regain her composure. Talking about her Dad had thrown her off-balance. Every time she thought he was in the rearview mirror, he virtually popped up again in her passenger seat and scared the holy bejesus out of her.

The mirror above the fireplace reflected her reality. Scared. Vulnerable. A little girl who wanted to be the strong, independent woman she had pretended to be in her formative years.

She closed her eyes and indulged in a dramatic sigh. In her heart she wanted to be the woman Jacob perceived her to be. Brave. Talented. Giving.

Could she let go, stop pretending, and just be herself?

If she fell back into the rut, she'd never been able to climb back out again. But how could she show Jacob her true self when she still didn't know who she was to begin with?

She craved his touch. Every ounce of her being desired what he longed to give and share freely with her.

The name of the last man who left her bed without a backward glance had long ago been forgotten. Jacob cared about her feelings.

He listened.

And for that reason, she loved him.

Oh, God. I love him.

Every nerve came alive, glittering in response.

She studied him while he hovered over the teakettle, waiting for the water to boil. His broad, bare back rippled whenever he moved. Board shorts hung low on his narrow hips. He was beautiful. A painted canvas, with bold lines, and in the shadows was a delicate softness. Even his hair, normally worn in a state of wild and wavy, softened and glowed under the kitchen lights.

His need to protect was gallant, in a gentle way.

She snuggled a little deeper into the throw when he approached with her tea. Mint and chamomile wafted around them and soothed her senses.

He turned the chaise lounge next to the couch toward the window. "There. We can watch the sunrise from here." He extended a hand to help her rise.

"C'mere," he walked with her over to the creamy leather lounge, settled, and made room for her between his legs. "You still look cold."

She climbed in between his legs, then he settled the throw around them.

She turned her head to listen to the beat of his heart. The bold, steady rhythm eased her muscles, and she adjusted her position. His legs and chest perfectly framed hers. He crossed his arms around her waist. "The sunrise should begin any minute. See the changes in the sky?"

"It's a magical time when both the stars and the sun coexist and allow each to live for a few more minutes before the other takes over."

"Is that how you see the world? Some element in the world must dominate the other? Why can't people be equals? Both living where needs and desires meet."

"That scenario doesn't exist. It goes against our ingrained survival instinct to dominate everything around us."

He grunted his disapproval, yet there wasn't any anger or disappointment. He simply disagreed. "Your point of view might be tainted." His thumb continued to doodle a circle on her skin. "When two people trust each other—respect each other—there isn't the need to put up protective shields."

"What you're implying is two people can coexist peacefully in the same space if love is part of the equation."

His small circular movement stopped. "I didn't say anything about love. My Dad tells Ben and me he loves us a lot, but deep down there is no respect. No trust. No, I believe if two people respect each other, no matter what their opinions are, then coexistence happens."

She let the concepts settle in the same way Dempsey circled his bed, scratching and pulling at the fleece before collapsing on a single spot.

She tipped her head back to look at his face. "Do you respect me, Jacob?"

He didn't answer her for a second or two, and her heartbeat stalled. He reached for her arm and brought her hand to his mouth, pressing it against her skin. "There's only one person in my life I've even admired more, and that's my mom."

Hope and thankfulness fluttered up from her core. "I respect you too."

And she did. If only she could figure out a way to control her irrational fears. She resolved as of that moment to reconcile with her past so she could start fresh.

"That's a good start, don't you think?"

"A good start."

He leaned closer, seeking her mouth. Rachelle held her breath. Her heart pounded in her ears. She reached for his stubbled face, liking the scrape against her skin, willing him to kiss her longer.

He created that little spark again. He felt right, good. Nothing in the kiss was fake. What she and Jacob shared was one-hundred-percent au naturel. She'd fought hard, but couldn't resist him any longer. His lips persisted, drawing out the kiss.

She turned to her side to give him more.

When he finally released her, he ran his fingertips through her hair and rested his forehead against hers. "I love the way you taste."

"It's my tea."

"I don't think so. I could kiss you until morning."

Her mind, still spinning from the kiss, couldn't think of any way to respond. He must have taken her silence as reluctance, because he started pulling away.

She slid her hand around the back of his neck and gently drew him closer, hoping, praying he'd give her another chance. "Kiss me again, Jacob."

He tipped her head back, then angled in, hovering just above her lips. "You're beautiful."

Rachelle pressed with her feet to scoot closer. "Then what are you waiting for?"

Instead of kissing, he reached and lifted her shirt, baring her breasts. She wasn't wearing a bra, so there was no barrier, and he didn't wait for her approval. He shifted her to the side to suck and tease and indulge.

"Oh, Rachelle."

"Don't 'Oh, Rachelle,' me. Don't you feel sorry for me," she yanked his head back and crashed her mouth against his. She didn't want his sympathy.

He leaned her back with a heated growl. "This isn't sympathy. This is admiration." He returned her angry kiss. "I want you more than I want to breathe. I want this." He used his powerful legs to pull them down the leather, switched their positions, and hovered over her. "Tell me no, Rachelle. Tell me you don't want this, and I'll stop."

"I want you. I want this."

He kissed his way down to her belly button. "Tell me again."

"I want this."

He rolled off the chaise, scooped her into his arms and devoured her mouth. "Hold on. We're going for a ride." He kicked the door to the guest room open and set her in the middle of the bed before kneeling on one end.

His fingers gently lifted the edges of her lace panties, and then with a pull, slid them down her thighs.

Rachelle gasped and reached for a handy Jacob body part. She wanted to touch, feel. He hovered over her and lifted, one hand on her ass, the other beneath her head. She angled her mouth to intersect with his.

His moan matched hers.

"Rachelle, you still have time to say no," he said between kisses.

"Touch me, Jacob. Don't stop."

When he again feasted on her nipple, she held his head for a second before urging him lower. And he indulged her, kissing her inner thigh, spreading her legs wider.

"Relax and let me love you, Rachelle."

Her muscles instantly turned to mush when he sought her core.

Yes. Yes. There. More. Ohmygod.

She pressed her head into the pillow and stretched her arms above her head, tingling with need, the need to have him deep inside her.

"Jacob? Please."

He didn't pretend to misunderstand. He was on a mission to give her pleasure, and the overachiever didn't disappoint. He kneed her legs farther apart, then tickled her core to open. But she didn't want to wait. She had waited for this day for far too long. She thrust her hips upward, to house him fully. Her inner muscles tightened around his eager erection, as his pelvic thrusts speeded up. Their mouths sought each other. She clamped her thighs around his waist as her climax gripped him, pulling him in. Seconds later, he came in a fiery burst of passionate groans.

The room awash in the smell of their lovemaking made her skin tingle with renewed energy.

He collapsed on top of her, holding her so tight there wasn't a bubble of air between them. Her heart boogied a happy cadence.

He slowly rolled to her side, pulling her with him and gathering her in his arms.

Her cheek rested against his skin.

The sun painted her colors on the bed and spilled reality into the room.

She'd made love with Jacob without any protection, without any hesitation.

What was she thinking?

Feelings and should-have thoughts waged war inside her head.

Wanting to feel a man want her for who she was shouldn't have stopped her from taking precautions. Then again, she didn't have one regret.

She wanted him.

He wanted her.

The situation didn't need to become any more complicated.

Jacob tucked a piece of hair away from her face. "What are you thinking?"

"I'm trying not to."

"Good. That's what I wanted to hear, because making love to you is better than any video game I've ever played."

Her body went limp and she started to laugh. "Is that so?"

Did he realize he couldn't have said anything more perfect? Did he realize she never thought she could love anyone—yet she loved him more than she thought possible? She should tell him, but the fear bug crawled up her leg and bit her hard.

Maybe she didn't need to tell him just yet.

Across the room, the fairy dust motes danced on the

sunbeams.

She wanted to frolic at that moment. Just be in his arms a little while longer. She closed her eyes against the what-ifs and maybes and let herself sink into his arms to hold off the future for just a little longer.

Chapter Nineteen

Rachelle gasped at the hotel conference room's splendor. The space had been transformed into a wonderland of color.

Mylar spaceships and strings of balloons hung from the ceiling. Tables were covered with purple and pink and blue and neon green tablecloths. The stage at the front held a massive floor-to-ceiling screen with rainbow balloon pillars on each side.

The kids will love this. Excitement fizzed along her skin.

She walked to the nearest table and picked up one of the plastic tubes of flavored sugar. Placards on the tables denoted wheelchair access. Ben hadn't missed a detail.

"Well, what do you think?" Jacob's hand firmly planted on the small of her back sent tingles up her spine.

"It's perfect. The kids will have such a great time."

A flash of movement made her turn, then relax. Ben sprinted through the tables at superhero speed.

"You're here. Finally." The panic in his voice raced out in front of him.

Jacob gripped the back of the nearest chair, as if bracing for bad news. "What's up?"

"All the food carts are in place. The staff has been briefed. The kids' goody bags are stuffed. The bakery delivered the cupcakes on time, but one of the hotel staff dropped several boxes. The cake is totally smashed." Ben took a half of a second to roll his eyes and catch his breath. "We don't have enough to fill the cupcake tiers."

His lips puckered with disapproval. "The videographer is here, but the photographer is stuck in traffic. Plus, Larson is MIA."

Rachelle surveyed the room and spotted the half-empty cake tier. "There's no time to get more cupcakes to match your theme. Is there a food warehouse nearby?"

Ben scratched his head. "There's one just down the street. What are you thinking?"

"If we get boxes of chocolate bars to fill up the tiers, that might work. The bars will be easy enough to grab, plus they won't overwhelm your party theme. Also, while you're there, you might want to see if they have those disposable digital cameras. If the photographer doesn't show on time, let the kids take the pictures."

"Sketch is there now looking for another cake. I'll text her." Ben grabbed the sides of her head and gave her a firm kiss. "Woman, you are amazing." He looked at Jacob. "You need to keep this one." He stepped back and looked around the room. "Now we just need to find Larson and complete the video game tests."

Jacob lifted his phone and started texting. Within seconds, he received a response. "Etch says Larson is here," he relayed, but his words were formal and stiff. "He and Etch are setting up the equipment for the video game now."

"Good. Good." Ben closed his eyes for a few seconds. "Very good." He opened his eyes. "Candy bars and cameras. Got it."

Ben's legs pedaled toward the back of the room.

A warm hand again slid around her waist. "Looks like you saved the day again." He looked ridiculously pleased, but she didn't know why.

"Your brother is doing an amazing job. It's not easy pulling off a kids' party, especially not one this size. When there are checklists for your checklists, the brain can go numb, and creativity can walk out the door. He just needed a fresh perspective."

"He is doing an amazing job, he always does, but you, lady, helped."

She opened her mouth, then closed it again, letting his praise heal her soul. She inched forward to appreciate his nautical scent. "This event is pretty special. The kids need this—same with the parents."

"I know what it's like to have a sick parent. There's fear from not knowing what will happen. I was always scared I'd get home from school, and she'd have been rushed to the hospital...or worse, she'd be gone. I'm happy I was there when the end came. I didn't want her to be alone."

"It must have been very hard."

"My mom and I talked about how she wanted her life to end. She was good about telling me when she was having good or bad days, never hid anything from me. Besides, kids are smarter than adults think."

"True."

His eyes, narrowed and focused on her face with a heightened level of intensity, sent chills cascading down her back. "I bet you were a smart kid. You figured out things well enough."

"I was raised to be a little adult. I didn't get much time to play." She cringed, knowing her spirited tone didn't entirely cover the brutal honesty.

"It's never too late to learn how to play."

From the look on his face, he wasn't talking about video games.

Playing with him was fun. In fact, they spent most of the morning rearranging the bed sheets—several times, in fact. But the intensity in the relationship made her uneasy.

She didn't doubt her love for him. He was a wonderful, kind man, but he could be overwhelming. She needed to pull back. Reassess. She'd gotten in way, way, way too deep already, and needed to swim back to the safety zone for a while.

Sure, Jacob was messy, fun, yummy, and gorgeous, and way too generous to be so rich.

However, her history had proved time and again if she didn't carefully choose her decisions, something terrible happened.

"Maybe we can play later," she almost laughed when his lower lip stuck out. "You have a party to throw and kids to make happy," she used the plausible excuse. She had learned from experience that it didn't take much to find a deserted room in a large hotel. When her father wanted her to close a deal, he made sure all possibilities were covered.

"Right." He tugged her against him, letting his mouth linger over her lips for a second or two. "Later." He stepped back and slid his hand around her. "I'll hold you to that, Rachelle Clairemont."

"Promise?" She teased with a fluttery wink.

"Woman, you drive me insane." He tugged on her fingers. "Let's go find Larson."

Her gut raised the caution flag, and she gently slipped an inch or two away. "Why don't you go? Drew's over there." She pointed with her chin. "Your designer texted me a few questions about my drawing, and we can chat while you do your thing. Besides, Glenn and his wife just walked in. You should go say hello."

"Are you sure?"

"Your team looks like they could use an extra set of hands."

He picked up a strand of her hair to play with the ends. "I appreciate you."

Her breath stalled. No one before Jacob had ever said they appreciated her, and he'd expressed his gratitude more than once.

The lack of appreciation might have been the result of her spending her whole life trying so hard to be extremely good at her job that she had disappeared, become invisible. Events just magically happened. But Jacob saw her, even when she was trying to hide.

"Thank you for being kind," Rachelle shifted. "You need to go. This is your event."

He ran his knuckles down her cheek. "I'll come back to find you. Ben saved you a seat up front."

Oh, man. His soft tone made her melt. "Go."

He kissed her nose and was off at a run. Intent on watching him race to the back of the room, she didn't notice a man sliding in beside her. When she turned, he was just there.

"Oh, I'm sorry, I didn't see you."

"No worries. I'm Ross, Ben's husband." She blinked a couple of times, getting her head around the word husband. He didn't look gay, but then again what did a homosexual look like? She mentally kicked herself for letting her former prejudices contribute to such idiotic thoughts.

"Is there a problem?" The playful crook of Ross's mouth, and the way his eyes danced with a good-natured humor, made her uneasy.

"No, no, um....no, problem. It's just I live in a small town, and..." She bit her lip and sighed. "No." She looked at Ross. "I want to apologize for my reaction. I was raised with my parents' prejudices. I'd like to think I've made some changes in my thinking, but it seems I need to work harder."

He leaned in. "Let me guess, three churches, two gas stations, and one street light."

Relief let her genuine smile sneak back into place. "Two churches, one gas station, and one street light."

His slow, melodic whistle said it all. "That big. Wow."

Wearing three-inch heels, she was tall, but Ross was taller—much taller. His long, lean frame, dark beard, and closely shaven head reminded her of last month's men's style magazine spread. His stonewashed jeans, brown suede shoes, and button-down shirt and sports coat were very chic.

She'd never been around anyone who was gay before Ben, and now his husband, and didn't quite know what to say, yet he didn't seem to hold her curiosity against her.

"Are you like Ben?" Heat burned her face when his eyes flashed wider. "I mean, are you a project manager type as well?"

A slow warmth spread across Ross's face. "Ben? A project manager? No. He's much too temperamental to be a project manager, but he does seem to keep Jacob on track, and that's what he's been hired to do." He trailed off when a hotel staff member dropped a tray and several people rushed to help. He shook his head and laughed. "I'm an intellectual property attorney."

Wow. Impressive. "Trademarks, patents, and copyright stuff. Correct?"

"You got it. Ben and I met when Jacob and Larson formed their company."

That must have been a while ago. She studied Ross's expression. "Jacob and Ben must be terribly disappointed in Larson." Her throat closed after the thoughts escaped.

"We're all disappointed. He's dropped the ball on this event, and other stuff." He rocked back on his heels. "I shouldn't have said anything. It's not my place."

His comments had drawn her in, giving her insight into Jacob's inner circle of friends. She liked Ross just as much as she liked Ben. Drew, Sketch, and Etch were different, and fun.

"Well," she tucked a strand of hair behind her ear. "It looks like everyone is doing a good job of picking up the slack." She pointed at Sketch following Ben to the tables with several bags in each hand. "The candy bars have arrived. Do you think they can use some help?"

"Definitely."

For a few seconds Rachelle just stared at Ross's easygoing smile. There was a twinkle of love in his eyes for his partner. She followed his gaze to Ben, who was racing around like his pants were on fire, his arms waving every which way. Ben's life was in a full-blown frenzy, and Ross stood beside her, stable as a rock.

Rachelle crossed her arms and leaned in closer to Ross. "I bet you two make an amazing team."

"We do. I love that man. He's a disaster, but I still love him." He laughed and shook his head.

Like all Jacob's friends, Ross was open and kind and welcoming. She didn't have to prove she was brilliant or capable. Whatever she offered, Jacob and those he had chosen to allow into his life accepted her.

Somehow she managed to fight back tears of joy. Being accepted for who she was, not the puppet playing a part, was a big dang deal.

She blinked rapidly to force away the sting of tears, because ruining her makeup on such a glorious day was not to be tolerated.

"Shall we?" Ross extended an elbow, then paused when a cluster of kids ran into the room. "I guess the party has started."

The room exploded with sound, so loud she didn't hear Ben approach.

"Rachelle, would you and Ross mind helping the kids find their tables?"

"Sure," she said, but it didn't matter. Ben was already on his way to deal with another crisis.

There were enough escorts, but Ben was making her feel welcome. Needed. Part of something bigger. And she appreciated his empathy for her situation—a stranger in a strange town, and an even stranger situation.

After forty minutes of getting kids and parents situated, she found herself waiting behind a young boy in the food line who was torn between which piece of fried chicken he wanted. A little girl in a fairy princess dress that perfectly complemented her cocoa-colored skin forced her way in between them, waving her wand and pointing to the giant cupcake tier.

When nothing happened, she tried again, doubling

the swirling efforts.

"What are you trying to do?" Rachelle asked.

"I would like a white cupcake, but I can't reach that high."

Rachelle pointed at the white cupcake with the gold crown surrounded by pink sugar crystals. "This one?"

The little girl, about four years old, nodded and then reached up with her hand outstretched, palm up.

"Oh, and you think if you wave your wand, a cupcake will magically appear?"

"Yep."

She dropped her hand, with a huff and a pout, evidently concluding Rachelle wouldn't help.

"Well, you know what they say, third time's a charm. Why don't you try again? And this time close your eyes."

The princess lifted her wand to make several dramatic swirls with her arm, then thrust her arms toward the table, the miniature wand in her hand still vibrating with the passionate effort. When glitter floated down from above, the princess's eyes opened wider, and her jaw dropped before she held out her hands to catch the glitter.

Rachelle brushed the remaining glitter on her hand off on the back of her pants, then stepped out of line to let others pass. She crouched down to eye level, bringing with her the white cupcake. "What's your name?"

The little princess shrank inward, looking down at her white patent leather shoes with a gold bow on the toe.

"Sarah," she whispered.

"Nice to meet you, Sarah. My name's Rachelle. Is this what you want?"

She peeked at the colorful treat, then nodded tucking her chin.

Rachelle's heart ached. She recognized the look. The trepidation of asking for what she wanted. The fear of wrath for presuming. She reached for the small hand, turned it palm up, and placed the cake in Sarah's palm.

When the child wrapped her fingers around the bottom, Rachelle dipped the tip of one finger in the white frosting and dotted the buttery cream sweetness on the girl's nose.

Sarah's eyes crossed, then a second later her face lit up with a joy so innocent and pure, Rachelle's breath hitched. The sweet sound of a child's laughter filled her soul.

"Are you two having fun?"

Rachelle glanced up to see the one man who made her laugh. Laughter was such a precious commodity.

Since the child had her hands full, Rachelle swiped the frosting off Sarah's nose and then stood. "Sarah and I were creating magic."

"I'm a princess," the four-year-old declared.

"Yes, you are. And so is Rachelle."

Sarah shook her head. "No she's not. Where is her princess dress?"

Jacob crouched down, chuckling. "Can you keep a secret?"

Sarah leaned closer, waiting for Jacob to reveal the precious information.

Jacob cupped his hands over Sarah's ears. "Goldilocks' dress is at home in the closet."

"Goldilocks," Sarah's eyes formed a perfect O as she stared at Rachelle.

He straightened, still holding Sarah's attention. "Are you staying to watch the video game?"

"No. I'm too young. My mom says I can't watch—it's too violet. I have to go in the other room."

"Violet? I think you mean violent, and your mom is probably right. But there's cool stuff going on next door. You can make a mask or draw."

"Can I make a hat?"

"I bet you can." Jacob winked.

"Cool. Let's go."

Jacob took a step to go with Sarah, but Rachelle

placed a hand on his forearm. "I can take her if you want. It looks like Ben needs you for something."

Jacob twisted his wrist. The Panerai watch, with its bold yet simple design, appealed to her sense of style, and apparently his.

"It's one o'clock. I bet Ben wants to start the presentation."

"Go ahead. Sarah and I'll check out next door, and then I'll be back."

"Be sure to sign her in at the crafts table. We'll keep track of her in case her parent is looking for her." Jacob offered a smile, but he was already mentally onstage giving his spiel.

Halfway out of the hotel ballroom door, a woman's frantic voice caught her attention.

"Sarah!" a woman with black-grey skin wheezed and reached for her daughter's arm. "What have I told you about wandering off, or talking to strangers?"

Sarah looked at her mom and shrugged. "She's not a stranger. This is Rachelle, and she's with him."

"Jacob Reyes?"

Sarah nodded and pointed toward the stage.

"Now, Sarah. What have I told you about telling stories?"

Rachelle touched her hand to Sarah's shoulder. "She's telling the truth, ma'am."

The woman shoved her daughter behind her.

"Jacob told Sarah a secret not more than five minutes ago. It was a special secret. Wasn't it, Sarah?"

Sarah peeked out from behind her mother's leg. "I told the truth."

"Yes, you did. And that was a brave thing to do."

Sarah hugged her mom's legs. "Am I in trouble?"

"No, hon," Sarah's mom rested her hand on the back of her child's head and nudged her closer. "I'm sorry for doubting you. I got scared when I couldn't find you, and I reacted badly. Will you forgive me?"

Rachelle reached her hand toward the woman, who was barely standing. "My name's Rachelle Clairemont, and you have an extraordinary daughter. May I escort you back to your seat, Ms..."

"Mary. My name's Mary. And thank you, Ms. Clairemont, for watching after my girl."

"It's Rachelle." She extended her arm. "And it was my pleasure." Rachelle glanced over her shoulder. "The presentation is about to start. Would you like to go next door and draw, or sit for a while?"

"I need to sit," Mary barely managed to force the words past her bluish tinged lips.

"How about this table?" Rachelle pointed to the nearest vacated oval table. "Would you like a glass of water?" Rachelle caught the eye of one of the nurses on standby.

"That would be nice. Thank you."

She settled Mary into the chair just as a nurse approached. Sarah's eyes had locked onto her mother as the nurse reached for Mary's wrist.

"And, you my little princess." Rachelle lifted Sarah's chin with her index finger. "Would you like to have another one of those cupcakes, to share with your mom?"

"A white one?"

"If that's what you want."

"Yes, please," Sarah sat up straight on her chair, swinging her feet.

Rachelle placed her hand on Mary's shoulder and squeezed. "Can I get you anything, other than water, Mary?"

Mary tapped her hand and started to cough at the same time. The worried look in Sarah's eyes was hard to miss.

"Okay, then. One magical cupcake and some water coming up." Rachelle winked and sent Sarah a smile and a bucketload of healing prayers for her mom. The nurse gave her the okay nod, which provided only a teaspoon of relief.

Rachelle walked toward the food tables with a couple of backward glances. Being a wife and mother hadn't ever been on the top of her list, but today made her change her mind. Jacob and this event made her want things she never thought possible.

A blast of music from the stage drew her attention.

"And, now, for our latest action-packed gaming video," Jacob announced while the lights dimmed. "My team has been working hard to present this never-before-seen video trailer. They created this just for you—because *you're* special—yes, I'm talking to you. Once it's over, relocate to one of the five gaming areas for more fun, and don't forget to get your goody bag full of toys and a special surprise. And now, since you didn't come here to listen to me talk, let's get on with the show."

She picked up Sarah's cupcake and started back across the ballroom. The stacked speakers roared with theatrical music. On the big screen, the emblem of Jacob's company appeared briefly before fading.

The next image churned the bile in her stomach. She stopped and looked around the room, but everyone else was looking at the screen.

The camera zoomed in on her animated face, with red eyes and black pupils to match the avatar's armor. Two-inch fangs emerged. The animated face that looked just like her hissed like a snake, then ducked in time to avoid double-sided blades slicing through the air where her head had been.

Rachelle couldn't breathe or take her eyes off the screen.

The she-warrior raced up the side of buildings and over rooftops, brutally killing everything in her path while being pursued by a handsome warrior who looked like Larson.

Seconds passed, and the warrior gained ground, getting closer and closer.

Jumping off a roof, the female avatar crashed through an open window and ran for the stairs barely making it through the door before an arrow whizzed past her head.

She turned to face the Larson lookalike.

Although the image looked nothing like her father, the years of feeling trapped, oppressed, never being able to escape, triggered an ingrained fear.

Her heart pounded. She couldn't breathe. Then the deathblow came, beheading her red-eyed lookalike.

For a second the conference room was absolutely silent. Then it happened. Her red-eyed lookalike's head tilted and rolled off her shoulders to hit the ground.

Cheers and whoops and applause came from all four corners of the room.

Her stomach lurched and the bile rose into her throat.

Leave. Now.

The cupcake forgotten, she ran to the sign-in table, grabbed her purse, and kept running until she made it through the hotel entrance doors.

Her lungs burned.

She fought for air.

Someone called her name. *Just keep walking. Don't look back.*

"Rachelle!" Someone grabbed her arm and spun her around. "Are you okay?"

Ross. *It's okay. Don't scream.*

"I need to leave."

"Okay. I'll take you back to Jacob's place. My car is in the hotel garage."

She shook her head. "No. I'm going to the airport." She plastered her purse to her chest like a shield to ward off an enemy and raised her hand to signal the next waiting taxi.

"What about your stuff?"

"I don't need it."

Not willing to wait, she briskly walked down the long drive. She raised her hand again. "Taxi?" *Please. Please.*

Please. Get me out of here.

"Just give me a minute, and I'll drive you to the airport if it's where you want to go." Ross touched her arm, but she yanked away. "Rachelle, you have to know already that the stunt wasn't Jacob's doing."

She wanted to put her hands over her ears, but she opened the back door of the taxi instead.

"It was Larson."

She nodded. "I know. It doesn't make a difference. I don't need any more drama in my life. I don't need this." She got in the taxi and reached for the door. "Please, tell Ben I'm sorry. He'll have to find a new designer for the house. I can't do it. And tell Jacob...tell him I'm sorry too."

She closed the door and pounded on the back of the front seat. "Please go. I need to get to the airport."

A debit card and a few twenties were all she had, but hopefully there was enough in her bank account for a ticket. If not, she'd have to think of something else. She was good at solving other people's problems, just not her own.

In the taxi's rearview mirror, she noticed the tears carving trails in her foundation and the cabbie's sympathetic eyes. She looked away, because she didn't care. Not anymore.

Her father had convinced her she couldn't make it alone in the world.

Maybe that's why she stayed with him.

Fear of the unknown.

She needed to stop blaming her father for her life. Because of him, she was stronger. Self-reliant. She wasn't afraid anymore.

But he was right.

There was no one to help.

She was alone.

She would always be alone.

But she'd figure things out. If nothing else, she was a

survivor, a she-warrior with impenetrable armor, battle-worn, but ready to fight.

Chapter Twenty

Jacob scanned the cheering crowd. The blonde racing toward the exit pierced his heart until rage kicked aside the hurt.

He promised to protect her, but it never occurred to him that he'd need to shield her from his best friend.

His hands balled into fists while a forced friendly smile fell into place.

The kids.

He needed to protect the kids.

"Wow, that clip was certainly not what I expected, but I hope you've enjoyed your time here today. Now it's playtime, so sign up for a playtime at one of the play station setups around the room and have a great time. And don't forget to pick up your goody bags on your way out."

He waved a salute and stalked off the stage to find Larson.

Fury honed and sharpened his senses. He caught sight of Larson and Etch just as they opened the employee exit door. "Oh, no you don't. You're not getting away—not this time." He took off running, hitting the exit bar with a blast of energy. "Larson!"

Larson lurched sideways as he looked over his shoulder, then turned, throwing his arm around Etch's shoulder so he wouldn't fall on his face. "Hey, buddy. Great job in there."

"Why? Why did you do it? Why did you change the program?" Jacob stopped an arm's length away from his partner to calm his urge to punch him.

Larson shrugged, but his feet kept walking backwards. "Dude, it was just a joke."

"Don't give me that shit," Jacob followed keeping the pace. "This wasn't about you just having a little fun—admit it."

Etch stepped forward. "Jacob, come on, take it easy."

"Not this time." Disgusted, he swallowed the rage while watching Larson struggle to stay vertical. "You promised to stay off drugs."

Larson licked his lips. "Okay. Okay. I'll stop. I promise."

Jacob snorted. "You couldn't stop now even if you wanted to. You're throwing away everything we worked so hard to achieve."

"Naw, man," Larson staggered backward another step. "I'm cool."

"Right. You missed the investor meeting, the design meeting, and now this."

"That bitch had it coming." Spittle spewed out of his mouth as his face reddened. "I'm the designer. Me." He pounded on his chest with his palm. "I make the game designs."

Jacob opened his mouth. Closed it again, shaking his head. "You're jealous."

"Am not."

"I can see it in your face. You're jealous because I used her designs at the meeting and shared them with the team."

"*I* design the games. That's what we decided. It's always been you and me against the world. Just you and me. We make the games."

Envy loosed on a rampage by drug use was what this vindictive behavior was about. Larson didn't like knowing someone else was important in Jacob's life. He wanted Jacob to himself. "Is that why you didn't show for the investor meeting—because I was bringing Rachelle and using her designs?"

"It was our meeting."

"Yeah, it was, but you didn't put together the designs we needed. You were too busy partying. We agreed on the deadline. You missed it."

"I was getting there." He scratched his chin and squinted against the light. "You should have waited for me."

"I couldn't wait, and the investors certainly didn't need to wait. Plus, I'm not waiting any longer. In fact, I bet you haven't even started the designs. Am I right?"

Larson attempted to flip him the finger, but he didn't have muscle control and couldn't get his fingers to cooperate.

"According to our corporate agreement we signed," Jacob's throat tightened, and he swallowed back his heart's resistance, "if you started using again, you'd be out."

Larson staggered closer to Jacob, weaving, but his bloodshot, glassy eyes intent. "You wouldn't do that. We're buddies."

"Fine. You check into a clinic today, and we'll talk about next steps."

"Fuck you, man." Larson shoved Jacob back, then pointed a finger at him. "Fuck you!"

Jacob shook his head. "I can't watch you do this to yourself again. I can't. You either get on a plane and check yourself into rehab, or I'll set up a new company, and you and I will no longer be partners." He studied Etch. "The same goes, Etch. I'll pay for you to go into rehab, on the condition you and Larson don't go to the same place. If you don't, you're off the team."

Etch bit her lip but remained silent.

"I'm sick of you being all high and mighty. You can't tell me what to do."

Jacob's heart ached. "You're right. I can't protect you anymore."

"Come on, Etch," Larson reached for the woman who barely reached his shoulder. "Let's go party."

"Etch," Jacob added a stiff warning to her name. "You need to make a choice now. If you walk out the door, you won't have a job, and I won't be able to help you."

Etch shifted back and forth.

"Don't listen to him," Larson tightened his arm around Etch's shoulder and turned her toward the exit.

"Etch?" Jacob pleaded. "Don't."

Etch ducked under Larson's arm. "I can't do this anymore. I can't be your party girl. You love the drugs more than you love me." She ran a hand down Larson's face. "Take Jacob's offer. We can get clean. Be together."

"No." Larson shoved her to the ground.

Jacob stepped forward, but he stopped when she waved him off. "I'm good."

But she wasn't good. He could see the tears pooling in her eyes. She shoved to her feet. "I love you, Larson. Since the first day we worked together, I've believed you're my soul mate. But the drugs have turned you into someone I can't reach or understand."

"The drugs help us create." Larson brushed away her explanation like a crumb on his shirt.

"No they don't. Drugs make our minds numb, dull. Have you looked at the stuff we've done lately? It's crap."

"Phst. You don't know what you're talking about."

He didn't care about her. He didn't care about anything—not anymore.

Jacob stepped between Etch and his buddy. "Come on. I'll call Courtney, and we'll get you on a plane."

Larson tunneled fingers through his unwashed hair. "You don't own me. You can't tell me what to do."

Rage engulfed Jacob. He couldn't help Larson. Not this time. The drugs had taken control, and the only thing Larson could feel was the need for more drugs. He'd lost. Lost his business partner. Lost his friend. Lost the ability to care anymore.

"Okay. You've made your choice." Jacob took a resolute step back. "Take care, Larson."

Jacob turned and took a couple of steps toward the ballroom, then looked back over his shoulder. "Etch, are you coming?"

She gazed at Larson for a long moment, then slumped, tears tracking down her face. "Yeah, I'm coming."

She shuffled along the long, tiled hallway littered with laundry and kitchen carts.

Jacob held the door open for her.

She stopped halfway through the door. "I do love him, you know."

Jacob's heart fought against his mind's decision to be apathetic. "We both love him, but we can't help him. He has to want to help himself."

When he saw her shaking with sobs, he opened his arms, and she walked into his embrace. "I'm glad you accepted my offer. I know it wasn't easy."

"I'm s-scared," she sobbed. "I got into a big f-fight with Drew and Sketch a few days ago. They both said I need to make a decision. They're planning to talk to you about it Monday."

Larson had already made his decision. Jacob stared back down the long, empty hall, wishing for a miracle, wishing the exit door would re-open, but Larson was gone.

Larson and Etch weren't the only ones who were scared.

He'd seen the way Rachelle took off out of the conference room, and he didn't blame her. He could only imagine her hurt and anger.

How could he explain?

He had promised to protect her, and now this.

"Come on." He gently guided Etch through the doorway. "Let's go find Ben and get you packed. You're not alone, Etch. We're your family. We'll be here for you.

You should feel good about taking the first step. It won't be easy."

"One day at a time, right?"

"One day at a time." Jacob spotted Ben and gave him an I-need-help look. Both Ross and Ben headed his way.

Ben studied Etch then him. "What's up?"

"You know those places we checked out in Arizona?"

"You mean the one in the desert?" His voice went flat.

"Etch says she needs a break. Can you ask Courtney to get her space in one of the facilities and make travel arrangements to get her there? Drew and Sketch might want to help Etch pack. It seems I need to do some explaining to a beautiful blonde."

"Then you better plan packing yourself," Ross added. "She took a taxi to the airport."

Jacob dropped his head, a roiling, nauseating mess of emotions drowning him.

Guilt. Hurt. Anger. Understanding.

"Okay. Let's get Etch settled first, and then I'll book a flight to Denver."

Ross put his arm around Etch and gave her a kiss on the head. "We've got this, kiddo. You'll be fine."

"What about Larson?" Ben asked.

A wave of misgivings swamped Jacob, but the feeling only meant he'd made the right decision. "Larson's decided not to join us. He's on his own now."

Guilt and grief tightened his chest, but he took a deep swallow to shake off the knee-jerk urge to blame himself. He didn't force Larson to take drugs. The only thing he'd been guilty of was covering for his buddy. Well, he wasn't covering for him anymore. If Larson wanted help, he knew where to find it.

He had a new company to build, employees to take care of, and a new designer to find. Although he had a good idea where he could find one.

The only problem was convincing her he wasn't the one who had just lopped off her head.

Chapter Twenty-One

Rachelle tied Dempsey's leash to the dog hitch outside of the Dreamy Delight bakery and scooted the provided water bowl a bit closer.

She clutched her portfolio bag under her arm as she opened the door and tossed a smile onto her face, even though she felt like someone had dragged her down the alley and kicked her until she was nearly unconscious.

She ached all over from the virus the lady next to her on the plane so kindly shared.

"Hey, Rachelle! What's up?" Jenna wiped her hands on her apron, then rushed around the counter to help Rachelle set the black leather bags she'd brought with her on a table.

Rachelle dropped her purse on the closest chair. "Don't get too close, you don't want my cold."

Jenna pointed over her shoulder. "Let me make you some of my defense tea. It's great for boosting your immune system."

"I'm good. I just stopped by to ask a favor. I have some artwork I was hoping you might display for sale. I know it's a big request, but..."

"Hey, what's wrong?" Jenna reached for her arm.

What isn't wrong? Rachelle pulled a tissue from her purse to wipe her nose and disguise her welling tears. She took a moment to stuff the tissue in a plastic bag and gather some courage. "My design job fell through, and I'm looking at other options." She placed a hand on the leather portfolio bag. "I have all this artwork I want to sell. The art gallery canceled my contract when my family name was the news headline for weeks."

"Art gallery. What art gallery?"

"It's a long story."

"I'm sorry. Your dad certainly made a mess of things. You know what your dad did has nothing to do with you. Right?"

"I wish other people felt the same way."

Jenna studied the oversized black case. "So what is all this? I didn't know you painted."

"I worked hard to keep my artwork a secret. If my dad ever found out, he would have forbidden me to paint again." Rachelle fiddled with a curly strand which had fallen over her shoulder. "I met a wonderful art instructor when I took an online class, and when she found out I lived nearby, she took me under her wing and let me rent the back room in her studio. The setup worked nicely. I could paint and store my stuff, and no one knew I was showing my work in her gallery. But I had to clear everything out at the end of last quarter."

"I see." Jenna's comment conveyed an understanding Rachelle appreciated more each day.

She pulled out the first 16 x 20 framed canvas and turned the piece over for Jenna to see. The baker gasped and clutched Rachelle's forearm.

"You did this?"

Rachelle studied the multimedia painting, which included fabric and other junk she'd found lying around the house. The strips of cloth gave the mountains their texture. Lace and small pebbles the riverbed. "Yes. It's one of my favorites. That's why I showed it to you first."

She reached to retrieve another large painting, a couple of mediums, and a few smaller pieces.

"Grant?" Jenna called. "Come look at what Rachelle brought in."

Grant appeared from the back of the store, rolling down his sleeves and buttoning his cuffs. "Hey, Rachelle."

Jenna took the canvas from Rachelle and held it up. "Look at this. Isn't it amazing? Rachelle wants to display her work for sale here. What do you think? My vote's yes."

Grant peered over his wife's shoulder. "How much do you want for a piece like this?"

Rachelle studied the lot. "How about three hundred for the bigger pieces, one fifty for the medium, and eighty-five for the small ones?"

Her gut clenched when Grant started shaking his head. *Please don't say no. Please. I need rent money, especially after paying cash for a plane ticket.*

He pointed at the large piece. "I'm thinking eight hundred for the large, three for the mediums. Hmmm. I'm not sure about the small, but I don't think you should undersell your work, Rachelle, because it's gallery quality. Once it gets out there, these pieces could fetch thousands. I'm not convinced eight hundred is a fair price, but Jenna and I have been looking for some artwork. What do you think? Will you accept eight?"

Ohhh. He loves my work.

"Yes. Yes. Yes." Jenna bounced up and kissed Grant's cheek. "I knew you would love this one."

Rachelle choked down relief, yet loneliness crept in.

A sting of tears threatened again, and she quickly imagined what her father would say about her selling her art. Anger cleared away the frail emotions in an instant. "I'd be thrilled to take whatever you want to offer."

"Done," Grant said.

"The name of each piece is on the back, along with a description."

"Perfect, I'll get the rest of these up on the wall this week." Grant lifted the stacked canvas, then nudged Jenna's shoulder. "What about Kyle?"

"What about Ky...ohhhh," Jenna turned toward Rachelle.

"Is your son okay? He's such a sweet little boy, and

he's been through a lot."

Jenna waved away her concern. "He's fine. Loves school. And he's growing like a weed. I think he has a crush on Brianne, Mara's little girl."

"Isn't she a lot older than Kyle?"

"Yes, but I think he has a crush on anyone with blond hair. Caitlyn, my sister and Kyle's mom, had beautiful blond hair. I was always jealous, because I was stuck with this mousy brown." Jenna giggled when she looked at Rachelle. "Kyle calls you the pretty bag lady. I was worried at first, but then he told me he thinks you're pretty and you have pretty purses. The red and black are his favorites."

"He has good taste. They're both Prada." *And if I get desperate enough I'll sell it to you.*

"He has an eye for art and style," Grant nodded. "We've been looking for a place to take him for art lessons."

Rachelle reached in her bag and grabbed her lipstick, which doubled as her adult pacifier. "I don't know. I haven't had time to develop a suitable curriculum for kids." *Or anyone for that matter.*

"Who else in this town knows how to create something like this?" Jenna paused two seconds. "No one. All the other artists hanging on these walls live miles away. You'd be perfect. Just let us know how much you would charge for the lessons. We had already discussed asking if you might consider private lessons."

"Oh, no." She applied another layer of lipstick to cover her fragile yearning for a child. "I can't charge you. You were the only ones who supported me after...you know."

"That's not true, but you should think about it. Kyle loves crafts and drawing, and there's no one in town who can show him art is more than crayons and paper."

"Okay. Stop. We'll start slow, and if he's still interested in formal lessons, then I'll teach him about light and color pigments."

When Jenna reached for her, Rachelle stiffened against the genuine, human hug, then tentatively touched Jenna's sides. "Silly woman. When you get my cold, don't blame me."

"It will be worth it."

"I hope you still feel that way when your nose is red and runny and you've gone through a whole box of tissues."

Grant lifted her pictures higher in his arms, the approval on his face tall and wide. No way could she doubt how he felt. He turned and headed for the back, then shouted back toward his wife. "Did you show Rachelle what you've been working on, Jenna?"

"Oh, yeah." Jenna rushed to the counter, picked up a tray of chocolate treats, and held them out. "Actually, you arrived at the perfect moment. I just created Rachelle's Indulgence, but I want to make sure you approve. I want you to have a cookie named after you."

Jenna held out the plate, beaming.

The old Rachelle would have dismissed having a cookie named after her as trivial. But the honor wasn't trivial. Not in Elkridge. The people Jenna considered worthy had bakery treats named after them. There were Ashley's Luscious Lemon Drops and Maggie's Marvelous Muffins, so why not Rachelle's Indulgences?

"There's only one problem," she clamped her teeth together, not wanting to hurt Jenna's feelings.

But didn't she promise to be honest with people? Then again, maybe she should just accept the honor and not say anything.

Jenna looked at the tray of exquisitely baked items in little paper trays. "What's wrong?"

"Oh, nothing is wrong. Everyone loves your treats. Forget I said anything."

She picked up a bite and shoved the round bit into her mouth, trying and failing to force the cluster of chocolate down. She wanted to gag, but smiled instead.

Jenna's eyes narrowed. "Look at you, you can't even swallow it, can you?"

"It's yummy," she lied her butt off and faked a swallow. "All gone."

"Open your mouth, then."

Rachelle shook her head.

A grin spread like hot oil in a pan across Jenna's face, and her giggles popped and bubbled to the point she had to set the tray on the table. "Would you like a glass of water?"

"Yes, please," Rachelle mumbled around the wad of sugar and flour.

Jenna giggled all the way through the kitchen and back again. "Here. Drink this. I put some fresh lemon in there to take away the taste." Jenna put her hands on her hips. "Now out with it. What don't you like about the cookie?"

Rachelle brushed her hair off her shoulder. "They are good, it's just...I don't like chocolate."

"What?" Jenna's eyes popped open with surprise. "When you had your real estate business, you ordered brownies and chocolate cookies every week."

"Everyone likes chocolate," *especially my father*, "and I ordered what they liked."

"I've never been able to figure you out."

That's because I've never been allowed to be myself. "One of our housekeepers used to sneak me potato chip cookies for my birthday. They were sweet and salty, and I loved them. I tried to make them one day, but they didn't turn out very well. Do you think you could find a recipe?"

"Sure. But you'll have to be the taste tester."

Twist my arm. "I keep forgetting you have diabetes. It must be tough being around temping treats every day."

"Not at all. Just like you, I love making people happy. You offer people chocolate. I make samples. It seems to me we're not too different."

The loneliness plaguing her for the past several days

began to slip away.

She had refused to return Jacob's texts and calls, making her feel even more alone. Jacob wasn't so different, either.

But, he had things to figure out and take care of—Larson being one of them.

She needed a clear mind and conscience to pinpoint next steps. Having a sexy geek with the overprotective gene around didn't help.

She loved him. Her mind and heart agreed about that, at least. However that was about the end of the collaboration.

She was determined to figure out how to be whole again, because if she couldn't, she wouldn't have any future with Jacob.

He deserved to have a full-fledged partner. Someone he could count on.

And she wanted him to be able to count on her.

However, her heart longed to feel his body pressed against hers. In the early morning hours she fretted about whether or not to send him a message and ask him for some time.

To wait for her to find her way.

But, she concluded, if he decided to move on with his life, then maybe their relationship wasn't meant to be.

At least that's what her mind kept trying to convince her heart.

"Thank you for being such a great friend, especially when I've given you no reason to trust me."

"You've given me plenty of reasons. Besides, I know what it's like to have nothing. But the best thing about nothing is you get to build your very own, personal something—and from this moment forward, your life will be yours."

"True." A peaceful calm settled over Rachelle's heart until a voice she never wanted to hear again, said, "Good afternoon, Ladies."

Rachelle slowly turned with her shield of indifference firmly in place. "Special Agent Bantner. What brings the FBI back to Elkridge?" Her nerves and the chocolate in her stomach lurched.

"Miss Clairemont, may I speak to you outside?" Bantner made a gesture toward the door.

Rachelle reached for her purse.

Jenna stepped in front of her. "Michael Bantner. I didn't think we'd be seeing you again. I don't mean to be rude, but when sex trafficking and drugs are your thing, it makes one nervous."

"Only sex trafficking." The man who had a personality taller than his size stood his ground, unfazed by her statement. "The DEA handles the drugs."

"Still," Jenna crossed her arms, creating a formidable barrier, but Rachelle didn't want Jenna, Grant, or anyone else to get involved.

"I'm ready." Rachelle scooted around Jenna and walked to the door, but Agent Bantner stood calmly, a mighty, rugged force in the fight against crime.

"No need to worry, Mrs. Graden. I just need a minute of Miss Clairemont's time, then I'll be on my way."

At the door, Rachelle turned with her pleasant façade firmly in place. "I'll be by in a few days to collect the art you don't think works in the shop. Thank you so much, Jenna. And Grant, too. I truly appreciate your help."

Jenna's eyes switched from defensive to serious. "If you need anything—anything at all—you know where to find us."

Rachelle nodded and hiked her purse higher on her shoulder. She retrieved Dempsey, took a deep breath, and made her way to the curb, tucking the dog in closer, needing the extra shot of comfort. "What can I do for you, Agent?"

He glanced right and left, making sure their conversation would be private. "Your father seems to think you can corroborate his latest story."

Her spine stiffened. "About?"

"About not having any involvement in tainting the heroin which caused nine deaths in Ohio. He said you have evidence of his innocence."

"Me?" Shock blasted adrenaline through her system.

Did he know about the log she'd kept?

Why did he involve her?

Then it hit her.

"I see." She reached into her purse for a pair of dark sunglass to hide behind.

Her father still believed he had control. Just like he always had control. "I believe I have what you need, but you'll need to give me a few days."

Bantner leaned closer. "You have until tomorrow." His spicy aftershave did nothing to calm her queasy stomach. "Don't try anything silly, Ms. Clairemont. We are watching."

"I'd expect nothing less from the FBI. You've never stopped watching, have you?" She let her blissfully happy smile slip into place, and she tossed her hair back like nothing in the world could be wrong with her "perfect," total shambles of a life.

Chapter Twenty-Two

Guilt scraped across Rachelle's conscience while she entered Jacob's home with the key he'd entrusted to her.

He wasn't home, thankfully.

She didn't want to be there any longer than necessary, and concentrated on getting in and out without him ever knowing.

The house held only bad memories—first her father, now Jacob.

No. No, that wasn't true. She wouldn't lump Jacob in the same category as her father. Jacob was an amazing man. She missed him, more and more each day. Craved his touch...longed to indulge in his salty essence. Loneliness gathered around, chilling her, but she'd have to deal with the Jacob issue later.

Right now, Special Agent Bantner and getting him and her dad off her back had become the priority.

Her dad relied on her. But today would end his parental control.

Tiptoeing along the tiled floor, she made her way to the laundry room—the one place the DEA and FBI hadn't searched thoroughly. Opening the sink's cabinet, she knelt to remove the trashcan and slide-out rack, then traced her fingers along the edges of the baseboard, searching for the small plastic tab. Pulling and lifting gently, she removed the false bottom of the cabinet and set the board aside.

The buried, fireproof safe had been her secret place since discovering her father had video cameras installed in nearly every room of the house, with few exceptions. He expected her to clean and do laundry when the staff was not available. He liked seeing her on her hands and knees scrubbing or ironing his shirts. Only his acts of control created a blind spot which she used to her advantage.

She turned the safe's knob left and right until her mother's birthday was completed and the lock clicked. The large plastic bag filled with small packets of pills and drugs sat near the top. Reaching in she lifted the bag and leather-bound diary filled with dates, times, names, and notes.

Lifting the false bottom board to replace it, she froze at the sound of footsteps.

"Rachelle? What are you doing here?"

The muscles in her back clenched, but she managed to shut the lid of the safe and slide the board in place.

"Jacob, I wasn't expecting anyone to be here."

"Obviously," he crossed his arms. "And what is that?"

He pointed at the bag of drugs.

An explanation was possible, but would he believe her? Did she want him to believe her? His overprotective genes would kick in, which was the last thing she wanted. She had no right to get him involved. He was a good man. He deserved better.

"I just needed to collect these things. I'll be out of here in a minute." She opened her purse and shoved the bag and journal inside.

"No. You'll tell me why you have a bag of drugs and a secret hiding place. Are you a dealer?"

"I know what this looks like," she rocked back on her heels to stand. "Jacob, listen. You need to let me leave, right now."

His jaw muscles rippled. "You're always leaving. Why did you leave San Diego?"

"Maybe we should talk about California another time. You're angry, and understandably so." She took a step toward the door, but he held out his arms to the side and moved to the center of the doorway.

"I'm not letting you leave until you tell me what's going on."

She tightened her grip on her purse handles, determined to finish what she'd started. "You need to walk away—now. Outside, right now, this house is being watched. If you don't let me leave, alone, you might be arrested."

"Me? I didn't have anything to do with those drugs."

And neither did I. An idea sprouted roots and began to grow. "Let me leave now, or I'll tell the sheriff these drugs are yours. He'll believe me. He already knows Larson was in town asking where he could buy drugs, and then he came here."

"Are you threatening me?"

"Yes. I'll tell the authorities I found a secret hiding place while I was remodeling." She gritted her teeth and raised her chin. She stood her ground and didn't dare budge. She loved him, and must make him believe. Acting a part couldn't be too hard. If she failed, he might find himself involved in something bigger and more complicated than he could possibly imagine.

"You wouldn't lie."

I just did.

"The sheriff asked about you when I was in town getting something to eat." He took a step closer, his arms outstretched. "Why, Rachelle? Why do you have those drugs? Why would you lie to the sheriff?"

To protect you. "Because I can."

"But we connected. I know we did. Rachelle... sweetheart."

"Jacob, don't." She couldn't breathe, her stomach coiling in tighter and tighter. Her hands shook. Her body ached. "Just let me leave. If you have ever felt anything for me, you will let me walk out that door."

She took a step, but he pressed a palm on the

doorjamb.

"What the hell is going on?" The hurt in his eyes heaped on another layer of guilt.

She straightened her shoulders, resolved to do what she knew was right. "Take care, Jacob." She brushed his hand aside and walked past him, but he grabbed her arm.

For a long while, she only looked at his fingers, praying he would release her. Finally the pressure eased, and he opened his hand. When she looked up, he was staring at her with vacant eyes.

"One question." His anger drew a dark line around his words, making them bold.

"Go on." She didn't dare look away.

"Did you feel anything for me?"

She could fib. Make up another story, and cover the truth. Hiding had become a habit, easy, but she wouldn't hide her feelings. He deserved the truth. "Yes. I respect you. Trust can be easily broken. Love can fade, but respect—respect is strong. Even in the worst of times, respect survives."

He stared at her. The only things moving were his eyes, searching hers for meaning. He was trying to see into her soul, but he couldn't. She'd gotten good at disguising her thoughts, her wants, her desires.

He was a fantastic man. The one thing good in her life. He made her look forward to her future—a future she just destroyed with another lie.

When he fully digested her answer, he nodded. "Tell me one more thing. Are those drugs yours?"

"No," she answered without hesitation.

He let out a shuddering sigh and took a step back. "Okay."

For some reason, he didn't question her further, and she was grateful. Yet the finality in his voice crushed her heart.

She had gone and done it.

Destroyed the one good thing in her life—to protect

him.

Tears burned behind her contacts. She placed the house key on the hook by the back door, then opened and walked out the door for the final time.

One day I hope you'll forgive me, Jacob.
I love you.
I always will.

Rachelle let her Mercedes roll to a stop and cut her engine. She peeked at her purse in the passenger seat. The black leather might as well have been a bomb, set to detonate in three, two, one.

Kaboom.

She reached for her Coach bag just as two black SUVs appeared in her rearview mirror. Before she could think, the assault team skidded to a stop on both sides of her car.

She was caged in—not that she planned to run.

Where could she go that her father wouldn't find her?

Agent Bantner opened the passenger door of the first vehicle and walked to her driver's side door as if it was a Sunday and he was strolling into the local church.

She grabbed her purse and slowly opened her door, making sure to keep her hands visible. "Agent."

He held her car door open, then closed it behind her. "Ms. Clairemont," he said in a tone still utterly formal and devoid of emotion.

Without a word she walked around him and up the steps to her cabin to greet Dempsey at the door. She left the door open to allow whoever was coming in to see there was no threat.

For once Dempsey followed her to the counter, hoping to get a treat. The bulldog was oblivious to the descending threat.

Agent Bantner entered, sauntered over to the small

oak table, and took a seat. He waited for her to fill the teakettle with water and place the pot on the hotplate. "Tea?" She asked, thankful the anxious tremble racing through her hadn't seeped into her voice.

He waggled a couple of fingers and shook his head. She chose a bag of chamomile orange spice, anticipating the need to settle her stomach.

She closed her eyes and felt the first rays of the sunset coming through the cabin shutters. The warmth of the sun touched her skin, but the chill of being alone and surrounded by overwhelming forces made her shiver.

When the teakettle whistle blew, she filled her mug and settled at the small table across from Bantner. Dempsey trotted over and curled beneath her chair.

Bantner's finger tapping sounded like the rap of leather-soled shoes on a tiled floor as correctional officers lead an inmate to execution.

She dunked her teabag in time with the thud-thud-thud. "I'd have a lawyer present, but I can't afford one since my assets were seized and bank accounts have been frozen along with my father's."

"Do you need a lawyer, Ms. Clairemont?"

A dry chuckle tumbled out at the anticipated response. So typical. "All my life, people have judged me." She took a sip of tea to test the heat level, then let the warmth and herbs soothe her nervous chill. "People saw the person my father wanted me to be. Very few ever saw the person inside."

"And who is that?" He missed nothing, not an eye blink, or a lip movement. He was good at his job, but she was better.

"A good person, Agent Bantner."

When she reached for her purse his hand clamped onto her wrist. "Easy, Ms. Clairemont. There's no gun in your purse, is there?"

"See? Now, that's what I'm talking about. I don't like guns, and I don't own one." She tipped her head toward her Coach bag with gold-toned treatments. "May I?"

His fingers slowly opened, and he inched his arm back.

She placed a pen and a notepad in front of him. "My dad wants me to corroborate his story, but I can't." *I won't lie to anyone, ever again.* "What I can do is give you the names of the men you haven't yet arrested."

"You're giving us names?" His disbelief was obvious.

"My father's lawyer locked up my immunity and advised me not to speak to anyone, and I haven't until now."

Bantner rested his elbows on his thighs and leaned in. "And why would you talk now? Like you said, you have immunity."

"I'm tired, Agent Bantner. If I don't tell you what I know, you'll be back a month from now, or a year, maybe longer. My dad will keep sending you back to me as long as he thinks he has control and believes I'll tell you whatever you want to hear."

"I see."

"I don't think you do." She picked up the pen and offered it to him. "Full immunity. I'll give you everything I have, and you go away, but I want your signature."

He leaned back in the kitchen chair, which was far too small for him. "I can't do that, Miss Clairemont. I don't have the authority."

She tilted her head and gave him a don't-go-there look. "You're bluffing. I saw your eyes twitch." Rachelle leaned forward and offered Bantner the pen again. "I haven't survived all these years without being able to read people, Agent Bantner. You have the authority, but that's not what I'm asking. I want your word."

"Mine." His intense gaze doubled down. "Why?"

"I watch people. Not what they say, but what they do. You're a man of integrity. You do what you say you're going to do. And because if you don't keep my name out of this completely, no matter what I tell you today, my life won't be worth much tomorrow."

He rubbed his lower lip with his finger. "Okay, Miss Clairemont. You've got a deal. Show me what you got, and I'll make sure your father never finds out about this meeting."

"Sign."

Bantner signed and dated the paper and shoved the notepad toward her. She picked up the pad, tore off the piece of paper, and handed the page to Bantner.

"You're not keeping it?"

"Nope. It's not legally binding. You know it. I know it. But at least now we have an understanding." She reached into her purse and plopped the bag of heroin on the table.

His amber-brown eyes widened with surprise, then filled with disappointment, then judgment.

"Don't be too hasty to condemn, Agent." She slid the bag toward him. "In this bag, you will find samples of heroin sold by my father. Each bag has a code written on the side for when the junk was packaged." She retrieved her notebook. "In this journal, you will find corresponding dates, quantities, and where the shipment went. People risked their lives for what's in this bag."

"People?" He accepted the book with a no-shit grin, then flipped the book open and scanned through the pages like he was flipping through a children's picture-book. "The book is in code."

"Yes."

He dropped the book and pulled the bag to him. "How did you get these samples?"

I can't tell you. "Does it matter?" Telling would put many lives in jeopardy, and she wouldn't break one more person's trust.

He selected a few packets from the bag and held them up to the light. "Regardless of the immunity order, you could have come forward. Given us this evidence."

She took another sip of tea, then set her mug down. "The DEA and FBI were looking for excuses to prosecute anyone with the name Clairemont. Plus, my father's lawyer hadn't worked out a deal."

"Still, this information would have been helpful."

"To you, maybe, but not to me. I needed an insurance policy. I wasn't sure my dad would demand immunity for me and my brother before he talked. Plus, I didn't know if you'd be willing to tie off the loose ends."

"I could still have you arrested."

"You could, but then my father would know I gave you this information. There are still people out there you haven't found. In this book are my father's connections. You need me to decode this book and prove whether or not my father is lying. The clock is ticking, Agent Bantner. Your look tells me you need this information. The sooner the better."

He let out a low sigh, clearly not thrilled at having his hand revealed. "Show me what you've got. I'll keep my promise."

"In time." She clutched her tea mug to keep her hand from shaking. "I need you to understand something." She swirled the liquid in her cup, watching it go round and round the edge of the rim. "These past few months, I've been thinking my life might have been easier in jail. Outside there's no metal bars and a false sense of freedom. There's the constant fear of not knowing what comes next. Not knowing when one of my dad's buddies will show up on my doorstep. I tried to leave when I was eighteen." She met the Agent's stare. "I didn't make it far."

The agent standing guard at the door sneezed, and Rachelle flinched. "Bless you," she murmured.

"Thank you."

His response challenged her mind to recycle.

The guard could have been a Madame Tussaud wax statue, complete with pressed blue slacks and an FBI windbreaker covered by a bulletproof vest, but he wasn't. He was just a man doing his job, who most likely wanted to go home to his family when his shift ended.

Bantner's eyes shifted for only a second to his agent, then back. "As I said, Miss Clairemont, you have my word. I will do what I can to ensure your name is not leaked."

"And my bank account?"

"I'll put in the paperwork to have the seizure lock lifted."

The small victory seemed insignificant compared with what she had to do to buy her freedom. She scooted to the edge of her seat and dumped out the bag of heroin, searching for three specific bags. She set them aside, opened the leather-bound book, then grabbed the pen. Ripping out a sheet of paper, she decoded the information, then handed the sheet over.

"Impressive."

She hadn't expected the praise. "I've been fascinated by ciphers since I was a little girl and found the need to invent my own. Sometimes I used to hide messages in my drawings and paintings. I always found pleasure in hiding things in plain sight."

"Your father underestimated you."

Rachelle closed her eyes, unwilling to accept the praise in his expression. "He always did," she whispered.

"If you ever need a job, call me. I might be able to hook you up with a consulting company I know." His generosity surprised her.

"That's kind of you, but I hope my days of living a double life are over. I want to discover who I am...or who I was supposed to be, anyway."

"Please take my card, just in case."

The cardstock, while ordinary, seemed heavy. She set it on the table.

"Rachelle, you already know who you are." He paused. "You're a survivor. You're strong. You're determined. I've no doubt you can accomplish anything you set your sights on."

A warming heat touched her cheeks. "Thank you, Agent Bantner."

"I have to ask, what about Jacob Reyes?"

Rachelle sat a little straighter. "He has nothing to do with this," she stated each word with a space to emphasize her conviction.

"I know he doesn't. He's clean as a dish fresh from the dishwasher." He leaned forward and placed his forearm on the table. "I have a guy still monitoring the house just in case our conversation didn't go as planned. He was pissed off after you left. Guys don't get angry at someone they don't care about."

"Did you read that in one of your training manuals?"

"I'd like to think I'm a good judge of character, and I think he's one of the good guys."

She reached for her mug twisting it around and around. "Is that so?"

"What's there not to like?"

She blinked, trying repeatedly to come up with something, but she couldn't. Not one thing she could find fault with. He was gorgeous, kind, wealthy, caring...he was even good with kids.

"Nothing, I guess," Rachelle admitted. "But why are you asking?" *More important, why should you care?*

"Just curious." Bantner stood. She dropped the little packets back into the bag while he watched. When she was finished, the agent at the door opened an evidence bag and sealed both the notebook and heroin inside, then handed off the bag and took up his station again.

Bantner held out his hand. "It's nice to meet you, Rachelle Clairemont."

A second passed before she slid her hand into his. "Michael."

A spark of laughter touched his eyes over the use of his first name. "Don't let your past dictate your future, Rachelle. You're still young. You can make a good life for yourself."

She walked him to the door. "That's what I'm trying to do, but sometimes it's not easy."

"The good things in life never are." He winked, then gave his team member an all-clear pat on the arm before turning back. "You have my card. Let me know how you make out."

She nodded, not trusting her voice. Slowly she closed the door. Dempsey trotted over and sniffed her feet.

Lifting him into her arms, she snuggled him close to feel the warmth of unconditional love. She inhaled a renewing breath, and prayed the current chapter of her life was finished.

"I think now I understand why my brother left you with me. He knew I would need you. If I ever see him again, remind me to thank him."

Dempsey licked her from chin to nose.

"Thanks." Appreciating how far both of them had come. "We need to decide what to do next."

Thoughts of Jacob sneaked in, but she had to squash those hopes. She had lied and threatened him. He was gone.

A few months ago she might have believed she understood loneliness.

Today she knew she didn't have the remotest idea back then.

The raw ache of loving someone and knowing they would never be back was agonizing. What was worse was knowing she had pushed him away—on purpose.

She needed a distraction.

The tin full of paintbrushes and paints sitting on the window ledge called to her.

The image of Jacob laughing filled her mind easily and vividly. She grabbed her sketch pad and pencil.

If she couldn't have him, she would at least have a memory.

Chapter Twenty-Three

Jacob closed his laptop and shoved away from his office desk to look out the window toward the baseball stadium. He loved the new office location. In the middle of the Gaslamp Quarter, the building had easy access to restaurants and shopping, and he loved being able to ride his bike to the office.

Not that he needed to work at the office.

He could work from home, like the programmers, but he wanted to build a place where everyone could hang out, collaborate.

In fact, he should be conferencing with his team right now. For the last few days nothing, not one idea had been generated.

"Want some coffee?" Ben asked, flopping down in one of his guest chairs.

"No. I'm good."

Ben crossed his legs and leaned back in the chair. "You sure about that?"

Jacob shoved his hand in his pockets but didn't turn around. He didn't want to see Ben's smug expression. "Leave it alone. I'm not going to discuss my trip to Colorado again."

"Oh, I don't need to know about your trip." Ben tossed a newspaper on his desk. "I know what happened."

Jacob glanced at the paper Ben tossed on his desk. The name Clairemont caught his eye, and he grabbed the newspaper.

Richard Clairemont indicted on additional charges.

Jacob scanned the pages.

New evidence uncovered.

Arrest warrants issued.

Unknown informant leads to arrests.

Rachelle. He paced the length of his office. *The drugs weren't hers. I should have known she told the absolute truth when I asked.*

But the additional charges didn't cover the fact that she threated to have him arrested. He dropped the paper on the desk and glared at Ben. "You don't know everything."

"I bet I know more than you do." Ben twisted Jacob's computer around, typed in a web address, then turned the computer in his direction.

"So what? It's a news briefing from the District Attorney about the arrests."

"You're not looking closely enough." Ben pointed at the courthouse steps.

Half hidden behind a pillar was a familiar face. Jacob moved the replay button back a few frames and froze the image.

Ben pointed at the screen. "Are you seeing what I'm seeing? Rachelle looks relieved. Not scared, or frightened, or upset—but relieved."

He started the video from the beginning. Indeed, she looked calm and relaxed, but she also looked thinner, almost gaunt, and the change worried him.

"So." He closed the laptop lid. "Her being there doesn't mean anything."

"Right. You're a storyteller. You study character and motivation. What would have prompted Rachelle to accuse you of selling drugs?"

"Nothing." His anger blasted into the room before he could find the emotional off switch. "She knows I don't do drugs. Even if she tried to convince the authorities the drugs she had were mine, she couldn't prove I sold them to Larson...or anyone else, for that matter."

"Exactly." Ben's expression told Jacob his brother had already gathered up the pieces, and none of them fit together. "Then why? Why would she threaten to tell the authorities? Think about it. What did you do when you found the prescription bottle in Larson's desk?"

"You know I covered for him, but the circumstances were different."

Ben crossed his arms. "Yeah, how so? You were protecting him."

Jacob paced by the window, his steps going faster and faster. "There's a difference. Rachelle threatened to tell them they were my drugs and have me arrested."

"For a guy who's smart, you're sure being a stubborn dumbass. Rachelle wasn't going to turn you in. She was carrying the evidence she needed to have her father convicted. You just happened to get in the way. The only thing Rachelle was doing was making sure you didn't stick your altruistic nose in where it didn't belong. You have a habit of helping people when it's not your job."

"I do not."

Ben started pounding his chest and coughing and gagging with laughter.

"Okay. Maybe I do try to protect the people I care about."

"Yeah, like Rachelle. She cares about you. She helped you with your presentation. She dropped everything to come to San Diego. She pitched in at the charity event to make sure it was successful. Do those things sound like someone who'd have you arrested?"

"You can't convince me she wasn't angry about the video game stunt. Having me arrested would have been sweet revenge."

As soon as the words were out of his mouth, he regretted the harshness. Rachelle wouldn't do anything just for spite. She couldn't. She'd been on the receiving end, and had too much empathy to do something spiteful.

He flopped down in the seat next to Ben. "Don't say it." He pulled his hands down his face. "I'm full of crap, and I know it."

Ben swatted at the bottom of Jacob's flip-flop.

"Hey, if it helps any, Ross thinks she was more hurt than mad, and he knows she wasn't mad at you. She said so. She'd already figured out Larson was behind the whole thing."

Jacob rolled his head on his neck. "Why are you taking her side?"

There went the boy-are-you-an-idiot laugh again. "I'm not taking her side. I'm always on your side. You deserve to be happy. And, admit it, Rachelle made you happy. You were different with her around."

"Yeah? How so?"

"For one thing, you slowed down. You don't slow down for anyone. With her you weren't thinking and planning and doing stuff 24/7. Drew told me you hung out at lunch, and even told a few stories. When was the last time you did that?"

Jacob turned toward the window. "I can't remember," he muttered.

"What was that?"

Jacob took a long, stoic breath. "You heard me."

"Yeah, I heard you, all right. So, are you just going to sit there?"

He shrugged. "She knows my number. She could have called. It's been more than four weeks." *Twenty-nine days and six hours, to be exact.* "I'm sure she's moved on."

"Right. The same way you have. You're stuck, like chocolate in peanut butter. You two go together, and you, dear brother, are as much in love as she is."

"But I've learned my lesson. I can't fix people. Larson taught me that."

"You haven't learned squat." Ben got up and stopped when he got to the door. "Rachelle doesn't need to be fixed or saved. Maybe what she needs is someone to be on her side for once. From what I've read, her father and brother never supported her."

"I thought we weren't talking about this anymore." Jacob relocated to his desk chair and did his best to look busy, hoping Ben would leave.

"Want Chinese for lunch? Ross is coming to meet me. We can all go."

He groaned inwardly. Ross and Ben were so gooey, huggy, gushy these days, especially since they finalized the paperwork to become foster parents. "I'm good. Drew and Sketch are stopping by later to go over some designs."

"Will you call her, or what?"

"Ben." He lowered his tone to emphasize the gruff warning.

"Okay. Okay." He held up his hands. "I'll drop the subject, but make sure you eat something today. Oh, and get out of the office. It's a nice day."

Jacob dropped his head to his desk.

"Okay. I'm going."

Jacob held his breath, waiting to hear the door close. When he heard the click, he exhaled heavily and picked up his cell phone. After a pause, he looked up Rachelle's number.

His fingers tightened around his phone as his throat knotted, and he tossed it on his open calendar.

The touch of her skin, the warmth of her kisses, her hair spread across his pillow...

He missed hearing her laugh. A laugh he heard only rarely.

Now he understood why.

"I thought I'd find you here."

Jacob squinted into the sun. "Hey Drew. Sorry I

missed our meeting. Did you and Sketch come up with anything?"

"No, man. Not yet, but we will."

He nudged his bike helmet aside to fish an extra towel out of his backpack and tossed it at Drew. "Take a seat."

Drew spread the orange- and green-striped towel on the soft white sand and flopped onto his back. "How's the surf today?"

"Not bad. One dude bit it a few minutes ago, but he's okay." Jacob stretched back. "What's up? And don't give me some nonsense about how you're here to catch some rays."

"And neither are you. You never just sit. Sitting around is for sissies. Isn't that what you're always telling us?"

"Call this research."

Drew's smile was double the size it should have been. "Okay. If research is what you want to call it." Drew brushed sand off his feet. "Sketch and I were talking. We were wondering if Rachelle might allow us to use a couple of her backdrop images." Drew lifted his ball cap and turned it around backward.

"That green one was good."

"Good? Naw. Her art is the bomb, man. Best art I've seen in awhile. Damn shame, Larson had to go and ruin it for everybody."

"Her leaving wasn't Larson's fault."

"When will you stop trying to protect him? He did the epic belly flop all on his own, and took Etch with him."

"Etch will be fine. She's getting clean, and I promised her a job once she gets out, as long as she signs up for random drug testing."

"Yeah, Etch will be fine, but I'm talking about you."

Jacob's eyes locked on Drew. "What about me?"

"You've been moping about this place for over a month. Why don't you call your pilot buddy and book it to Colorado?"

"Don't you start. Ben's already been on my case today."

"Good."

Jacob dug his toes into the sand, hoping the cooling grains would ease away his growing frustration.

Drew rocked him sideways with a nudge. "Seriously, man. Rachelle's a helluva woman. And her artwork. What I wouldn't give to have her on the team."

Jacob lifted his phone out of his nylon bag. "You think what I showed you before was good? Check this out." He turned his phone sideways for Drew to see. His long-time friend shielded the screen to see the images. "These are gnarly. Are they new?"

"I got these a couple of days ago."

"There's more?" Drew accepted Jacob's phone and right-swiped through the images. "Amazing. If you don't want her, how about I ask her out?"

Jacob grabbed for his bike helmet, ready to swing, then stopped. What was up with that? If he didn't have feelings for Rachelle, why did Drew's question make him want to clock the guy?

He leaned back and let the sun soak into his skin, but he could swear he caught a whiff of her scent. He scanned the beach...but no, she wasn't there. Just some other women walking by. Drew suddenly became distracted.

"Why don't you go chase bikinis for a while and leave me alone?"

"I'm not going until you promise to set things right." Drew rocked back, stretching his muscles. "Why don't you invite her out here for a proper vacation?"

The idea pumped him full of oxygen before deflating. "Not a chance. You and Sketch will kidnap her and put her in a dark room and make her draw for hours."

"Hey, it's not torture if it's what she loves doing."

Creating art is what she loves.

He could set her up, help her get started. Heck, he could even hire her. *Damn it. There I go again, barging in to help.*

He had to learn how to be in someone's life without helping, or worse, trying to fix everything. Rachelle nailed it when she said he couldn't help her—that all he should or could offer her was respect.

He respected Rachelle, and loved her even more.

"Fine. I'll text her and see if she wants to do some work for us."

Drew wrapped his arms around his shins, an agitation twisting up his face. "That's why we're both still single, dude."

"What? I said I would text."

"My point. She won't respond."

"You don't know that." But, his buddy was right. "Everyone texts these days."

"Butt cheeks, you're missing my point."

"I didn't miss squat. I get what you're saying."

"You'll go see her, right?"

Jacob let his hair flop and blow across his face. "Maybe."

Drew's arm shot out and toppled him over into the sand, and he laughed when Jacob tossed sand over his shoulder.

"Stop your nagging and get out of here. Let me enjoy the sun."

What was up with everyone? His cell phone buzzed and Sketch's text popped up. "Going out with a coupla friends. Want to join us?"

He groaned. "Now Sketch is trying to set me up."

"Oh, yeah, man. I forgot to warn you."

Jacob rolled to his feet. "You're right. I need to get out of here for a while." He picked up his blanket and made sure to shake it downwind.

"That's my man."

"I was thinking Hawaii." He laughed at Drew's disappointment. "Just kidding."

"If you want some company, let me know. I heard the

bike trails at the ski resorts are scorching."

That's all he needed—a giant kid to babysit.

On second thought.

He was through trying to protect those he loved.

Drew was on his own. Rachelle had helped him see not everyone could, or should, be saved. People had to want to be saved. While others wanted to figure out the right path for themselves.

She taught him a good lesson, and he was better for it.

He'd be an even a better man if she would just return his darn texts.

Chapter Twenty-Four

Rachelle watched the second hand circle the clock face on the wall.

Mr. and Mrs. Sutter should have arrived five minutes ago. Because of their tardiness, Rachelle suspected the couple only wanted the free vacation and weren't interested in buying a timeshare property.

It was a job, and she was grateful to have one, even if she hated being behind a desk ten hours a day. The property company out of Chicago loved her, especially since she was local and could help visiting tourists envision Colorado's four seasons, show them around town, and make them feel at home.

In the past month, Elkridge had come alive.

Others might not have noticed, but she had. Or maybe she had changed.

The sun streamed in through the blinds and landed on her desk. The blue sky with fluffy white clouds floating by made her daydream. She imagined jumping on one of those clouds and riding off to find her dreamland of unicorns and magical fairies and dragons.

A welling softness came with the image of Sarah in her princess dress and a cupcake in her hand.

She fished her sketchbook out of her purse and opened it to the last sketched page, Jacob's half-finished face.

What are you doing? She chided her heart for thinking there was even a hope he might one day come strolling into the office and sweep her off her feet.

She tapped the pencil on the pad of paper, annoyed with herself for giving the time of day to such irrational thoughts.

Why would he come back? She lied to him.

She hurt him on purpose..

When the sales office door opened, she stood and smoothed her skirt down and grabbed her marketing portfolio.

"Oh." Her surprise lifted then deflated.

Tony Gaccione walked in carrying a ginormous pink, purple, and white bouquet. "Rachelle. I have a delivery for you."

She studied the arrangement, then her desk calendar. "Hey, Tony. I thought Blooms swapped out the waiting room arrangement on Mondays."

"That's what the contract says, but these are for you. We got the wire order this morning."

She accepted the foot-tall vase. "There's no card. Who are they from?"

Tony's shrug made her muscles tighten. "The order was anonymous, and Blooms doesn't share billing information."

Her nerves began to twitch. Her father always sent her flowers, especially when he'd forced her to do something she didn't want to do.

She inhaled the glorious scent of fresh flowers. "These are pretty. Did Gina make the arrangement?"

"Yep." The pride in his voice was unmistaken. "This arrangement is my wife's favorite."

"Thank you for coming all this way to deliver them."

Tony tucked a clipboard under his arm. "You're welcome." He turned, then hesitated, then turned back. "You know, there's been a lot of talk around town about you lately."

Rachelle grabbed the back of her chair. "I suppose there has."

His forehead creased and his mouth settled into a

frown. "People say you've changed. I didn't believe them. You've always been a snotty bitch..." he shifted the clipboard, "...but I can admit when I've been wrong. I'm sorry for dumping you into the hamper and rolling you into the guys' locker room."

In my cheerleading uniform, no less. "If my brother hadn't been spreading those false rumors about me trying to get Gina kicked off the cheerleading squad, you wouldn't have done it."

"You weren't trying to push her out of the squad?"

Rachelle chuckled. "Why would I do that? We wanted to win the state cheerleading competition, and she was the only one small enough to toss in the air who could also land safely."

"Your brother is a jackass."

Her protective heart closed ranks. "Growing up with our father wasn't easy. Let's just say my father didn't like my brother's rebellious streak, so he made sure Brad was raised to be 'a proper man.'"

Her former high school classmate looked as thoughtful as she'd ever seen him. "For what it's worth, I am sorry."

"Me too," she murmured.

Tony took a step back, turned, and then was gone. The silence expanded into suffocating.

"Sounds like your life hadn't been easy."

Her head snapped up. "Jacob! Wha-what are you doing here?"

"I'm looking for a real estate agent. I have a property to sell."

He's leaving. The hope in her heart did a kerplunk. "I see."

"I'm not sure you do."

She reached for her sketchpad and closed the book. "Then why don't you explain?"

His broadening smile entranced. "You see," he paused by the edge of the desk, "I've recently discovered the house holds bad memories, and I want to sell it."

She took a deep breath and swallowed the devastation. "Well...the market is strong. As a real estate professional, I must advise you, though, that you might not get your full value, since you've only held the property a few months."

"I don't care about the money. Only my girlfriend's happiness."

Girlfriend? What girlfriend? He'd moved on. She felt like the ground beneath her feet had shifted and dumped a mountain of rocks on her. "You're not coming back?"

"I didn't say that. I also want to find a new place that meets my girlfriend's needs. She's a designer, and she'll need a studio to create her art. In the master bedroom, there needs to be two closets. One for her and one for me."

A designer. Was Jacob dating Sketch? She couldn't see him dating Etch. Another notch was sliced out of her heart.

His oversized smile expanded. "Maybe a couple of kids' rooms, and a game room."

"Of course. A game room complete with surround sound and a movie theatre screen." Did he know he was ripping her heart out? "I have a concern."

"Only one?" Why was he smiling? This wasn't funny.

"You wanted a quiet life. With all those people living in the house, you might not get the quiet life you wanted."

He pressed his palms flat on the desk and leaned in. "I believe my needs have changed."

"I see."

"You could still do the magazine spread I promised." He straightened.

"Magazine?" she asked. Hope flared.

"I can't sleep. I can't eat. I can't write. I want you in my life."

"Wait. Are you trying to say you need me?"

"No. I said I *want* you in my life. I've learned I need to

be less codependent, less enabling, and more supportive. Both you and Larson taught me that."

Me? Does he mean me? He couldn't mean me. "I've missed you."

"I've missed you too, Goldilocks." He took his time walking around her desk, then picked up a strand of her hair. "Sweet Goldilocks."

His eyes mesmerized her until her righteous conscience gave her a good kick. "But you shouldn't have come."

"Why, because you think you might put my life in danger?"

Rachelle stared at Jacob, not sure whether she should breathe or exhale. Should she hope? With each passing second, her soul filled with anticipation.

"You really shouldn't be getting involved with a person like me—I'm afraid I'll always be dealing with my past and father's indiscretions."

A slow smile creased the corners of his eyes. "Are you still trying to protect me, Rachelle?"

She nodded slowly, finally understanding his smile. "How did you figure it out?"

"Ben figured it out."

"Ben." She picked up a pencil and rolled it between her fingers. She fought the urge to close the distance between them and jump into his arms. Instead, she let him come a little closer...until the scent of the ocean suffused her with a sense of calm. She tugged the flower arrangement closer. "Are these from you?"

"Please tell me there are no other guys in your life sending you flowers," he whispered. His breath brushed across her skin. His lips hovered over her mouth.

"There's no one but you."

His mouth gently touched hers, and she desperately wanted to indulge, but she had to stop him from making a mistake. He didn't need her past dragging him down. She placed a hand on his chest and pressed.

"Jacob, we shouldn't be doing this."

"By this, do you mean kissing?"

"Are you selling the house because of me? You like that house. I can tell. You're talented and wealthy and have plans. You need to focus on your future, and I need to focus on mine, which is a bit unstable at the moment."

"I don't want a future without you."

She tried to swallow, and when that didn't work, she tried to exhale past the knot in her throat. "Yes, but you have such a promising future. I can see the headlines now, fans are raving about the latest video game released by Jacob Reyes. There's nothing like it on the market. It's a must have on every kid's Christmas list."

"There's just one problem with that headline." He tucked a strand of hair behind her ear. "You didn't include your name along with mine."

An agonizingly slow tickle of awareness sneaked up her spine. She studied his face. "You want me to work for you?"

"No, love."

She squeezed her eyes shut, disappointment shutting her down.

"Rachelle. Look at me."

She slowly opened her eyes to see an intent and beautiful face.

"I don't need another employee. Nor do I need an assistant. I need a partner—a life partner." His eyes softened. "Scratch that. I need you. Your love, wit, charm, support. Only you. I need you." His raw honesty filled the room to the point there was nothing else he could say.

He'd opened the door to her heart. Years of barricading her feelings and ideas and thoughts fell way. He pulled her in and held her close. Safe. He reached in his pocket, and took a step back, lowering to one knee.

"What are you doing?" She reached for his arm, but he moved it out of reach.

He turned her hand over and placed a tiny spaceship

on her palm. "Rachelle Clairemont, I want to explore together. Create together. Would you be willing to come aboard?"

She lifted her hand to get a closer look at the tiny spaceship.

"I want us to reach for the stars," he tugged on her hand. "What do you say?"

The look on Rachelle's face was transparent, and the openness was all Jacob needed to know for absolute certain he'd made the right decision.

His mom had been right. He had money and homes and friends, but nothing compared to the pure joy and love blooming in her eyes.

She reached for him, clamping her fingers around his shirtsleeve, dragging him closer.

"You gave me a starship," she whispered against his lips.

He nodded, nuzzling her neck, then her collarbone. "What do you say?"

Her violet eyes were glistening with glory and melted his heart.

"Are you sure you want a co-captain? Not a first officer?"

He leaned in and kissed her nose. "Don't you think you've spent enough time hiding your talents? How do you know what you can truly accomplish if you're not free to explore?"

"You want me to create?"

"I want you to do whatever your heart wants to do, as long as it's with me."

Her hand trembled when she touched his cheek. "You are the most amazing man, Jacob Reyes."

"You're pretty incredible yourself, Rachelle Clairemont. Now, is that a yes?"

"Yes," she responded without the hesitation or doubt or negative feelings that usually surfaced when she said yes to a man.

When the office door opened, she groaned. "My appointment's here."

"You don't like this job?"

"Hate it."

He caressed her cheek, then cupped her cheek. "Then quit."

"I still need to pay rent this month. I can't quit."

"Yes, you can. You can do anything you set your mind to."

She stifled a laugh. "Now?"

"Right now. This second."

The joy from the early moment rebounded. This man, this kind and gentle and wonderful man, made her incredibly happy. She was free. Free to choose. To make decisions. She blinked back a tear.

"Miss?" The couple waited in the doorway. "Sorry we're late. We're here for our appointment."

She looked at the couple, who were in their late sixties, and wearing tennis shoes, jeans, her with a sun visor, him with a baseball cap. Both were a little tentative. They definitely were there only for the free snack.

"Tell you what. You don't look like you want to spend twelve hundred dollars a year in timeshare property taxes and fees, so why don't we skip the tour and I give you your certificate for a 3-day, 4-night stay at one of our exclusive resorts? It will save you an hour and a half of time you can use to poke around Elkridge, possibly stop at the bakery for a nice treat and latte."

The wife looked at her husband, slack-jawed. He wasted no time. "We'll take it."

Rachelle opened her top drawer and pulled out a packet and signed the bottom line. "Here you go. Have a great vacation."

The couple grabbed the packet and hit the door faster

than a kid racing out the door for recess. Jacob looked at the closing door, and then her. "Well done."

She edged around the desk, a bit hesitant. "Thank you for forgiving me...about the arrest thing, I—"

"It's okay. We're good. As long as you promise never to lie to me again."

"Never, ever again. I promise."

"Do you respect me, Rachelle?"

"Of course I do," she said, and then felt her face heat with delayed understanding.

"I respect you too. You once told me trust can easily be broken and love can fade, but respect always survives." He wrapped his arm around her. "I respect you, but I also love you."

"I love you too, but I never dared hope you would love me back."

"As you'll soon find out, when I commit to something, I'm all in. Come on. Let's get out of here."

She inched back, her eyes darkening. "Where are we going?"

"Wherever you want to go."

The sensual spark in his eyes caused a blanket of goose bumps to spread across her body.

"If you don't want to go back to the house here, we could fly to San Diego, or—"

She pressed her fingers over his lips. "Let's go back to the house. I want to check out some rumors I heard around town."

"Rumors? What type of rumors?"

She opened her desk drawers, shoved the few personal items she had into her purse, and walked around her desk.

He leaned in to kiss her as he settled the vase and bouquet in the crook of one arm.

"If the rumors are correct," she said demurely, "your new bed arrived. Are you interested in taking it for a test drive?"

His eyes darkened. "Several."

Chapter Twenty-Five

Rachelle inspected her updo in the floor length mirror and adjusted the crystal pins holding the long strands in place. The wedding dress would come next, but she asked Jenna and Etch for a few minutes alone to decompress from the morning's activities, and to reflect.

Her hands shook with anticipation.

Everything from Jacob serving her breakfast in bed, to the makeup artist and stylist doing their thing on the back deck while surrounded by all the women she was coming to know, to the delivery of her flowers.

All perfect. All precious.

Never did she allow herself to dream this big before.

Jacob loved her, the woman she was on the inside. The person she wanted to be.

A noise made the reverie stall. The guest bedroom window slid up, and she turned just in time to see a body nosedive and roll into the room.

"Jacob?"

Panic welled, and she whipped around to make sure her wedding dress was still hidden inside her closet. She crossed her arms over the lace underwear that was supposed to be a wedding day surprise.

Her fiancé jumped up from the floor and closed the window.

"What are you wearing?" she asked, letting the shocking image sink in.

His tux jacket barely covered his Spiderman boxers, but his matching socks... The laughter started slowly and spread until she was holding her stomach and doubled over. "Where are your pants?"

"Ben took them. I wanted to make sure you are all right, but he started ranting some bullshit about omens and not being good luck to see the bride, so he took them and wouldn't give them back."

"I must say, Mr. Reyes, your socks are mighty fine."

"If Dempsey gets to wear a Spiderman outfit for the wedding," he altered his stance and jutted out a foot with a perfect toe point, "I get to wear matching socks and undies."

"And they both go so well with your black patent leather shoes, but they are not as fine as my shoes."

She slid her four-inch heels out from under her floor-length slip to show him her red-crystal-covered shoes decorated with black crystal spider webs and two-inch spiders.

His eyes flared with lust. "Oh, woman. There's a reason I'm marrying you."

And that sexy I'm-in-love look was the reason she loved this man. Every day would be full of adventure, laughter, and more love than she could have imagined.

"Stop. Don't come any closer." She thrust her hands in front of her. "I know what you're thinking, and you're going to ruin my hairdo or makeup. The photographer still needs to take pictures."

"The hairdresser is still here. She can fix any damage."

She laughed at his playful grin. "No." She pointed toward the window. "You need to leave. I need to finish getting dressed."

"About that." His face grew serious. "I realized as I was getting ready I may have rushed you a bit on this wedding thing."

The first warning of trouble gripped her stomach. "Four weeks wasn't a lot of time, especially with a house remodel thrown in. Are you having second thoughts?"

"About you, absolutely not. About the wedding,

maybe."

A jubilant sigh flicked off the warning light.

He reached for her hand. "I know you said you wanted to keep this house." His gaze travelled over the guest room with new furniture, paint, and décor. "But the house does hold some bad memories."

"That's why having a wedding here is perfect. We get to create new, happy memories. I designed this house from the door pulls to the bathroom tile. I got to pick every element of the design. Plus the back deck at sunset will be the perfect backdrop for the wedding pictures."

"Are you sure?"

She grabbed ahold of his lapel and tugged him closer, taking in a whiff of his breezy scent. "Always worrying about others, aren't you?"

"I want today to be special."

"It will be special. I'm just sorry your dad and stepmom can't be here." She straightened his boutonniere and then stroked her hand down his white pleated shirt.

"Ben's not. He's pissed about dad cheating on his mom. Neither want to be in the same room, and neither of us need the drama. Our friends are here. That's what is important." He tenderly ran a finger down her arm. "Love the silver sparkles on your skin. You smell good enough to eat."

"Slow down, mister. I'm looking forward to standing at the altar with you in your Spiderman briefs and matching socks."

He leaned in and kissed her nose. "I love you, Mrs. Reyes."

"Oh, yeah?" She slipped a wide smile into place to soften the mood. "How much do you love me?"

After a millisecond pause, a smile matching hers stole across his face. "You are worth more to me than my entire comic book collection."

A warm thrill ran all the way up from her toes. "That much, huh?" She kissed his cheek, and then smudged in the Spiderman red lipstick she'd searched hard to find. "That's a lot, but I love you all the way to the Milky Way and back."

"And back?" His brows lifted. "Stellar. I feel like I've just found the Holy Grail."

She leaned in just as the door to the room crashed open.

"I knew it." Ben stood in the doorway with Jacob's pants slung over his forearm. "Out! Now!" He pointed toward the hall.

Jenna stormed into the room with a look that should strike fear into anyone in her path. "Tell me he didn't see the dress."

Rachelle stepped in front of Jacob to shield him from the fury. "Don't neuter him. He didn't see anything."

"Except the shoes that were supposed to be a surprise," Jenna corrected.

Rachelle stuck out the tip of the high heels to admire them once again. "I do love these shoes."

"Holy crap. Those shoes are the bomb." Etch rushed closer, then studied Jacob's legs. "No offense, boss, but I think she outdid you on this one."

"That's no surprise. You ladies always outdo me."

"Enough talking." Ben pushed Jacob into the hall. "The wedding is in twenty minutes." He reached for the door handle and pulled, but at the last minute poked his head through the narrow gap. "Love the shoes," he winked, then was gone.

"Thank goodness he didn't see the dress," Jenna retrieved the gown from behind the door. "At least there will be one surprise left."

Rachelle ran her fingers over the intricately beaded, formfitting bridal gown with red waist trim gathered just above the waistline and a crystal spider brooch drawing the eye. The matching two-foot train of satin embroidered with intricate spiders hidden among delicate flowers and spider webs completed the look. The calla lily and red rose bouquet would complete the ensemble. "It's definitely one of a kind."

"I'll say. Even your veil is perfect." Etch lifted the lace hairpiece from off the dresser.

Rachelle accepted the veil and bent to place and secure the combs in place. She studied Etch in the mirror. "What's perfect is you in that dress. I'm glad the treatment center allowed you to come to the wedding. It wouldn't have been the same without you." Her newly found friend glanced down at her dress.

"I never thought anyone would get me in one of these things." She stuck out her high-top tennis shoes. "At least you didn't force me to wear them heels. I would have wrecked the wedding when I did a face-plant."

Rachelle slid a hand around Etch's shoulder and forced her in front of the mirror. "I said you didn't have to wear a dress or get your hair done, but look at you. I must say I love the red spikes." Rachelle patted the top of Etch's Mohawk. "It's the new you."

"It's the new me, thanks to you and Jacob. Thanks for coming to visit."

Rachelle shook her head. "It was all you. You did the hard work to be here, and I couldn't be more thrilled you decided to be my maid of honor."

Tears welled in Etch's eyes.

Rachelle reached for a tissue. "Oh, don't do that. You'll get us all started."

Jenna gathered up the train of the dress. "Etch, can you help?"

The two women gathered up the fabric and slipped the satin over Rachelle's head. A second later, Jenna zipped up the fabric and then began fluffing the skirt.

Tears stung her eyes, but she forced back the emotions. "Jenna? Etch?" Both women stopped fussing, poised to fulfill her every request. "Six months ago, I didn't think I had a friend in the world. Life looked pretty bleak. I had no job, no money, and then you both reached out to me and offered me your friendship when you could have turned away. But you didn't. For that, I will always be grateful."

"Well, crap," Etch pressed a tissue to her eye. "I was trying hard not to lose it." Etch glared at Jenna. "How are you keeping it together?"

"I've been focused on where to find some Superman briefs for my husband. My-oh-my." She fanned her face. "Sexy didn't even describe the placement of the—"

"Tell me you were not looking at my husband's ass."

Jenna's cheeks bloomed a cherry red. "Well, I'm not dead, you know."

"Oh, I know. All of the women in town have nothing to talk about but your sin-sugar frosting."

"I gave you a jar of every flavor." She licked her lips with a wink. "I'd try the one with the spider on it first. I made a special batch of white chocolate with bing cherry flavoring."

"That's it." Rachelle picked up her skirt. "Let's get this wedding over with. I'm ready for the honeymoon."

Jenna rushed to open the door. Etch walked into the hall as Rachelle followed.

At the door, Rachelle paused and looked back at her old room. She'd spent hours in her room, staying out of her father's way and daydreaming about her future.

She couldn't have imagined one better than this.

She was in love with a man of her choice, surrounded by friends she adored, in a house she had helped design and build.

A house she intended to fill to the brim with love.

Chapter Twenty-Six

Eleven Months Later

Rachelle slid her hand into Jacob's and squeezed to give him strength while she looked out over the local crowd buzzing with excitement.

Jacob raised his hand and the voices quieted. "Thanks for coming today," Jacob's voice boomed out into the gathering. "I see a lot of familiar faces, and others I've not yet met, but would like to get to know. Today is a day of healing and a day of celebration. Today is the opening day of the Larson Center for Creativity." Applause and cheers infused him with peace and a sense of rightness. "Hours and hours of hard work and volunteer efforts have gone into making this day possible."

Jacob's grip tightened. "Our goal was to build a place for Elkridge kids to gather, explore, create, build, write...the possibilities are endless. I believe we've achieved our goal."

Another round of clapping and cheering prevented Jacob from continuing, even though Rachelle understood he wanted to hurry up and get through this day.

"Our goal, with the support of this community, is to provide every child with a place to dream."

Rachelle could feel Jacob fighting to breathe, and snuggled a little closer.

"Feeding a child's dream is important. Larson, my best friend, believed in dreams. His biggest dream was to build a game every child, no matter where in the world they lived, could play. He too achieved his dream, which is why he donated the funds to build this very special place."

The rawness in his voice made her ache. She wished she could take on his burden, but she couldn't. No one could.

"So..." he brushed the melancholy aside, "let's fulfill some dreams, shall we?"

Ben and Ross pulled open the freshly-painted red doors leading into the small brick house. The kids who were in the front rushed up the newly-built, disability-accessible ramp to be the first inside. Jacob walked through the crowd shaking hands and accepting several back slaps. She stayed with him, step by step, never leaving his side. When he'd shaken the last hand, she let him catch his breath.

"Would you like to go in?"

"Not yet." He looked like he was trying to swallow a rock.

"Is there anything I can say to help?"

A small suggestion of a smile lifted the corners of his mouth, but his heart wasn't behind the attempt.

"I can't stop thinking about what Larson's letter said. I've read the lines a dozen times, but some of it is still incomprehensible. I have no idea what he was trying to say." He hung his head. "I want to know. I need to know what he was trying to tell me."

"Jacob, don't torture yourself." Rachelle slipped her arm around his and rested her head on his shoulder. "He made his choice. You need to stop asking why. There is no answer. And even if you had the answers, you'll never get all the answers you want to hear."

"He said he'd accomplished everything he dreamed of doing." Jacob's jaw muscles pulsated. "That he was tired of fighting off the demons and couldn't fight anymore. But that wasn't true. He had so much more to give."

"That was the drugs talking, not Larson."

"I know. It's just I wanted him to get better," he whispered. "I needed him."

"You're not the only one who needed him to get better. Drew, Sketch, Etch, Ben, Ross...the list goes on and on. He would have been surprised at how many people attended his memorial service. Letting the kids play his video game at the service was inspiring. No one could have given him a better tribute than you did."

"It was your idea," he kissed her forehead.

She tightened her arms around him, trying to support him with her love.

"I'm sorry your dad couldn't come today."

"Someday he'll realize what he's missing, but I can't worry about him. He's not my responsibility."

She stroked his face. "Look at you, being all psychological and rational."

"It must have been all the family sessions I sat through with Etch."

"Hey, you two. Aren't you coming in?" Etch skipped down the ramp, but her red, splotchy skin told a story she probably didn't want anyone to read.

Rachelle allowed Etch to enter the circle of kindred spirits. "We're just taking a minute to honor Larson's memory."

The computer designer's face pinched, magnifying her grief. "Yeah, well, he was a selfish ass. He should have had the balls to stick around." A flood of tears pooled in her eyes and spilled over.

Rachelle wrapped her arm around the woman quickly becoming her best friend. "He would have been proud of you. You're still sober. You're making the changes necessary to stay clean."

"I was scared shitless when my substance abuse counselor told me I couldn't go back to San Diego. It freaked me out. But she was right. Same friends. Same habits."

"The town sheriff is doing whatever he can to keep

Elkridge the cleanest town in the state. Besides, you living here, helping run Larson's Center, makes sense. I can't think of anyone better. The kids love you, and you've come up with some fun programming. Larson would have approved."

"Yeah, but the parents aren't thrilled about having a former addict around their kids."

Rachelle squeezed Etch's hand. "With time you'll win them over. I've learned the hard way that this community can be very forgiving."

"Still, it's a bit far away from Drew and Sketch. I'll miss them."

"I bet you won't," Jacob interrupted. "I'll hook your place up with a satellite, and I've ordered a high-speed Wi-Fi and telepresence conferencing room to be installed there. It'll be just like you're in the same room with Drew and Sketch and the rest of the team."

"No way. Really?"

"Consider it an advance. I'm going to need you to work your butt off before the next investors' meeting. They're expecting a live demonstration."

"I'm cool. I've got plenty of time before ski season. Did I tell you I'm taking up snowboarding next winter?"

"Promise me you'll wear a helmet." Jacob was clearly troubled by Etch's eye-roll. "Maybe I should take out an extra insurance policy."

"Don't worry, I'll be careful. They say boarding is just like surfing. Rach, you should try it."

"I don't think so." Jacob's arm slid around her waist and squeezed.

Etch swatted Jacob's arm. "Didn't you say something about being less protective? Letting people do their own thing."

"Skiing while eight months pregnant? Now this I'd like to see."

There was a pause. Then—boom—Etch's face lit up like a kid who'd just been told they were taking a trip to

Disneyland. "You're pregnant? Really? I'm going to be an auntie?"

A laugh rippled up and exploded with joy. "I was thinking more along the lines of godmother."

"Me?" Etch jammed her fingers through her short, black hair, then let the strands fall over the razor buzz on the side. "Seriously? But I'm a screwup."

Rachelle reached for her friend's hand. "Look at me. I don't want to repeat myself." She pursed her lips. "You and I, together, we are going to put the past behind us. We are strong, amazing women who deserve good things."

"Well said," Jacob kissed his wife's cheek. "I'm surrounded by amazeballs. Now, ladies, if you don't mind, there's a ten-year old inside who says he's gonna cream me at Exlander."

"Criminy," Etch laughed. "Did you happen to mention you created the game?"

"No. There are certain things you can teach the kids, and certain things you have to show them."

"And if you lose?" Etch asked with a straight face.

Rachelle held her breath, wondering which way the conversation would roll. One-one-thousand. Two-one-thousand. Three-one...

Jacob's shoulders began to shake with a much-needed gust of relief. "Then I'll be the one learning the lesson. Like I always say, find a kid under the age of fifteen, and they'll teach you anything you need to know about the newest gadgets."

"Why fifteen?" Rachelle asked.

"They can't drive yet, and most still think the opposite sex is pretty lame, so the latest trends are their focus."

An idea swirled into Rachelle's head. "Why don't you hold a game designer contest for kids? The winner gets a three-month design contract. What a great way to find early talent."

When his mouth captured hers, thoughts of kids and

games flittered right out of her head. He eventually leaned back. "There's a reason I married you."

"I have good ideas and wore a Spiderman dress for our wedding?"

"That and because you give great kisses."

"All right, you two," Etch pushed on their shoulders. "Cut it out. We have work to do."

"That's what I hired you for," Jacob leaned in and brushed his mouth over Rachelle's again, then deepened the kiss. He sucked in her bottom lip before releasing her. "I suppose we should go in."

"It's okay if you take another moment."

"I miss him." Jacob picked up her hand and kissed her palm, then held it against his chest. "I keep checking my phone to see if I have a text from him. I could love him, but all the love and money in the world couldn't save him."

"Everyone tried, but I'm not sure he wanted to be saved."

"He taught me how to love better."

She placed a hand on each side of his face. "Your love doesn't have to be prefect, it just has to be honest."

"Well, Mrs. Reyes. Know I love you. Respect you. Trust you. Is that honest enough for you?"

She brushed her thumbs across his cheeks. "I love you too, Mr. Reyes. And there is nothing I would like better than to take you home and show you how much, but I would never, ever want to stop a young man from humbling my beloved husband."

"Is that so?"

"That is so."

"Well, Mrs. Reyes, just you watch. Aliens can't mess with my tribe. I'm going to annihilate the enemy and save the world."

I wouldn't expect anything less, my love geek.

Thank you for reading ATONEMENT

Up next is *BITTERSWEET*

From award-winning author, Lyz Kelley...

She survived to return to him, only to find him dead.

Leza was looking for her best friend and found love.
But she'd already committed to going undercover to crush a sex-trafficking ring.
Each day memories of Sheriff Sam helped her through another day.

She returns to the small town to get married.
But Sheriff Sam is dead.
Life is unjust and cruel.

Heath had his whole life planned until his sister's death.
Forfeiting his career as a Marine, he returns stateside to adopt his niece.
Life as a single-father and deputy is demanding, but then he meets Leza.

She's a challenge.
She intrigues him. Make's him feel. He wants her.
She's vowed never to love a lawman again.

Tragedy strikes forcing both Leza and Heath to take another look at what they desire most.

Look for the next book in the Lonely Ridge Collection coming the fall of 2018.

If you're interested in learning about my new release, check out my website or sign up for my newsletter at **www.LyzKelley.com** and get a free book for signing up.

I'm so glad you could join Rachelle and Jacob on their journey to their happily ever after.

Those of you who have read my books or been part of my newsletter have heard my explanation for why Authors never see their Star Ratings requested by Amazon, so thank you for allowing me to share the information once again.

When Amazon asks a reader to "Rate this book" on their Kindle or through an Email, Amazon is the only one to see these ratings.

I'm left clueless about how you feel about this book. Your input matters.

Book reviews help me decide what kind of books I write. Plus, the more people who leave an review, the more likely Amazon is to move a book up in the rankings? Written reviews help other readers find and love a series.

Please continue to rate the book on your Kindle or reader or through your email as this helps Amazon, but take an extra moment to pop over to the review section and leave a few words! Seriously, a few words like, "great story," is enough.

If you have not read my Elkridge Series or the Lonely Ridge Collection, and have no idea why authors keep asking you, as a reader, to take a few minutes to leave even a couple of word reviews, here's the break down of how reviews work in this crazy business.

Reviews (not ratings) help authors qualify for advertising opportunities. Without triple digit reviews, an author may miss out on these valuable opportunities. And with only a "star rating" the author has little chance of participating in specific promotions, which means authors continue to struggle, and many talented writers give up writing altogether.

Readers aren't the only ones who use reviews to help make purchasing decisions. Producers and directors use your reviews when looking for new projects.

This is why asking for your help.

A few kind words make such a massive difference to me. Your words give me the encouragement I need to continue writing because honestly, I write my books for you, and I'd like to keep delivering the types of stories you want to read.

And, yes, every book in a series needs reviews, not just the first book. Even if a book has been out for awhile, a fresh review can breathe new life into a book. So, please take a few minutes to leave a short review. Even a couple of words will brighten my day.

Lastly. Thank you for reading this book. I hope to see you again soon. Cheers!

~ Lyz

Award-winning author Lyz Kelley resides in a small community in Colorado with her husband and several four-legged family members. She's a disaster in the kitchen, a compulsive neat freak, and tea snob, a lover of board games, gardening, and painting. She loves writing about strong women who have endured challenges and the men who enrich their lives.

Lyz loves hearing from her readers!

Email: Lyz@LyzKelley.com
Newsletter Sign Up: www.LyzKelley.com
Facebook: Facebook.com/LyzKelley
Twitter: Twitter.com/LyzKelley
Instagram: Instagram.com/LyzKelley
Goodreads: Goodnreads.com/LyzKelley
Bookbub: /Lyzkelley

 Belvitri
Services
www.Belvitri.com

www.LyzKelley.com

54045064R00138

Made in the USA
Columbia, SC
28 March 2019